A Daughter Betrayed

BY

SHAD'E ZUIWETA

Table of Contents

DISCLAIMER.. v

ACKNOWLEDGMENTS vi

INTRODUCTION.. vii

PROLOGUE 1

CHAPTER ONE 1990....................................1

CHAPTER TWO A NEW ENVIRONMENT..... 10

CHAPTER THREE BEFORE VICTOR 22

CHAPTER FOUR 1992 30

CHAPTER FIVE WHERE WERE YOU WHEN I NEEDED YOU?...39

CHAPTER SIX BATTERED AND BRUISED ..48

CHAPTER SEVEN ENVIOUS.........................60

CHAPTER EIGHT TORN 70

CHAPTER NINE DIAGNOSIS.........................83

CHAPTER TEN ST. FRANCIS BLUES 93

CHAPTER ELEVEN A PRISONER IN MY FATHER'S HOME 99

CHAPTER TWELVE 2010 112

CHAPTER THIRTEEN THE CHURCH MEETING: PRESENT SITUATION 118

CHAPTER FOURTEEN GRANDMOTHER CARA 126

CHAPTER FIFTEEN ALL IN THE FAMILY . 133

CHAPTER SIXTEEN BLOOD ISN'T ALWAYS THICKER 148

CHAPTER SEVENTEEN INJUSTICE 156

EPILOGUE 165

ABOUT THE AUTHOR 170

Disclaimer

A Daughter Betrayed is a novella inspired by actual events to raise awareness about child abuse and narcissism. Any resemblance to actual persons, living or dead, events, or locales is entirely coincidental. The opinions expressed are those of the characters and should not be confused with the author's.

ACKNOWLEDGMENTS

I would like to firstly thank the man upstairs, God, for allowing me to breathe and for making all things possible even when some had not believed in me. I thank my husband Ryan, as well. You have been so supportive throughout everything when I never had much support from those who said they would never leave my side. To my children, mommy loves you so much. I dedicate this to you and so much more. You are beautiful beyond measure!

INTRODUCTION

There are many adults today who still suffer at the hands of their parents. Sometimes it is because of what happened to them as a young child. Not all parents are created equal. Most possess a narcissistic personality, a disorder that affects over 150 million people today. These types of parents can be jealous, making others feel guilty for the things they have done. They lack empathy. They covet power and praise, rooted in a sense of entitlement. Sometimes, playing the victim within the legal system is a tactic used to get what they want. Belittling is a hobby that they do to others, even to their own children.

This is A Daughter Betrayed.

PROLOGUE

"Even if my father and mother abandon me, the Lord cares for me." Psalms 27:10

The cordless phone sitting on my table rang loudly, stopping me before I walked out the door for court. I rushed over to pick it up before the fourth ring.

"Se'Atkins residence?"

"My God, Tamara, you were right! I'm so sorry I didn't believe you about your family!"

Elise, a long-time friend of my family, who I trusted and tried to turn to for help early on, continued bellowing into the phone with several more apologies. I could tell something had just transpired, and it bothered her greatly.

"Calm down, what's wrong?" I asked, easing down in a seat at my dining room table. "Is everything okay?"

"Your people have been calling me all day trying to find out where you're living," she replied with a nervous tone. "And they want to know if the children are with you. I told them I didn't know, so they've..."

"What? They've what?"

"They've been harassing me."

Elise had gotten a small taste of my pain. She hadn't believed me when my parents had falsely reported me to the child protective services agency, accusing me of child abuse. Not only did I feel I'd lost my family but her as well.

Now, feeling distraught by my parents continuously harassing her, she didn't know where to turn. Sometimes, you don't see the truth in things until it happens to you. She told me that though I was like a daughter to her, taking my word to inform the police of the matter would be too much. She had been close to my family for a long time, and she was afraid. Therefore, she had chosen sides, and it wasn't mine. For the life of me, I never understood what I did to deserve such hatred and abuse from my parents. I had been born into a family that chose to look away from their arrogance and pride. Rather than take me by the hand and pull me up from that ledge I was slipping from; instead, I was left hanging, to fall in ways I believed at one time I could never rise from.

The people that I believed in and trusted the most, my blood, tugged at my legs. I felt myself falling forward as they tried to pull me further into the depths of sorrow. I slept with one eye open, not knowing who my parents would call next to come knocking at my door from the harmful lies they spilled.

My name is Tamara Se' Atkins, and I was a prisoner from childhood to adulthood for many years until I chose to break free from my parents. They made it known that no one leaves them. I admit, I wasn't fully prepared for a fight against my narcissistic father and co-dependent schizophrenic mother, but I had to be. I went so far as to change my name through the courts to keep myself free from their wrath. It did no good. All the things my parents did to me, still those closest neither listened nor believed me when I spoke out. No matter where I relocated to escape them, they were determined to find me. My father wanted to ruin my reputation, to make me out to be someone I'd never be in front of the world. I've come to terms that not everyone wants you to be happy. Many will go to great lengths to sabotage that.

Whatever happened to real loving parents? In the real world, many of those don't exist. I wondered *why did I keep dancing with the demons that were trying to make me bleed?*

CHAPTER ONE

1990

There it was, the new Barbie and Ken dream camper set that was sitting beautifully on an oval glass-shaped stand of a shopping window. It was in a Toys R' Us store, and it seemed to be calling my name. My eyes glinted in the light, then a flicker of emotions came over me. I didn't have any dolls to play with, so normally, when we came to browse the store, I'd test out some of the new toys and beg my mother for anything with the Barbie logo on it. Back then, I asked for what a lot of seven-year-old girls my age would ask for instead of the electronics kids rave about today.

I tapped on my mother, Evelyn's back. From her reaction, I could tell she already knew what that meant.

She turned to me and yelled, "Tamara, would you please stop!"

She placed my hands at my side and pointed between my eyes. "Stop asking me for that damn toy! You know I don't have the money."

Saddened, I replied, "Yes, ma'am."

My mother always told me that she either couldn't afford the toys I wanted or that I had to ask my father, Lawrence Sr., who wasn't around much for the things I wanted. I tried my best to understand our misfortunes, although sometimes, I really didn't as a child. Most of the toys or clothing that I received came second-hand. If any were new, then those items mainly came from my Aunt Kelly. I was hoping my mother would stop by the Forsythe Park down on Sycamore Street during the bus ride home like she usually did with my brother Lawrence and I, but she didn't.

When we arrived at our small apartment at the Wilshire in the city of Monroe, Louisiana, I rushed to grab the very last banana pop in the fridge before Lawrence could. Though our father came and went most nights from time to time as he pleased, he was paying for the apartment we lived in. My parents found themselves downgrading to the lower-income parts of the city to keep afloat or to keep us from living on the streets. It was never easy as a child being awakened in the middle of the night with your brother to gather your belongings and dip out before your parents' landlord showed up the next day to collect three months' worth of rent that was long overdue.

There was constant thumping on the walls, and the neighbors could be heard blasting their loud music, engaging in arguments and fights, either inside or outside the complex every night.

We skipped most dinners, sometimes eating canned foods just to survive until our father brought along groceries, then he'd leave the house again and be gone for several more days. My mother didn't have a clue where he went. She never worked, and I never knew why when we struggled badly. Maybe it was because she'd been so depressed or just didn't bother. When our father didn't come through as she'd hoped, she ended up going to the welfare office, and we waited until the food stamps rolled in. After I finished the banana pop, I went to my room and noticed a hamper full of laundry overflowing to the floor. I ran back out and took my mother's attention away from the dirty dishes she'd been cleaning.

"Mama, could you please wash my laundry?"

She dried her hands and looked at me. Her eyes were intense, swirled with angry red. "If laundry isn't given to me in time, then you'll have to wear the same dirty underwear until laundry day comes back around."

I should've known she'd respond that way. It was like I got the lesser treatment- the short end of the stick. I would just have to make do with what I had. I was always mocked and ridiculed by classmates, the fact that I rarely got any new clothing as they did. My family knew we didn't have much by the dreadful appearance and utterly weary look on my face when we visited for the holidays.

I awoke to sharp hunger pains, like knives, stabbing me in the gut. I called out, "Mama, my stomach hurts!"

I held on tighter to my gut, wishing the pain to stop, but the growling wouldn't let up.

"Mama!" I shouted once more. I walked into her room, moaning and tugging at the ends of her violet gown as she sat on her bed.

She sprung in the air and responded, "Dammit Tamara, did you forget what I told you before?

I'm doing the best that I can around here. How come you can't be more like your brother?"

"I'm sorry, Mama, I forgot," I responded tearfully.

I went back to that small bedroom where my bed waited for me in the room I shared with Lawrence. Tears stained my cheeks, and the hunger panged my stomach. I could feel it boiling like a pot on a stovetop. I could tell my mother was sad about our father. Her loyalty to him had her believing in his promises when he hadn't been around. She was dependent on him for many things that he'd later use against her in their arguments.

Grandmother Helen decided to visit and stepped inside our apartment wearing a sheer polka-dotted neck scarf wrapped firmly around her neck, hair in a long-braided ponytail and a butterfly hair clip she favored. She was my favorite grandmother, always so sweet and dear to me, but it seemed my brother had been her favorite. She sat down to have a cup of coffee with my mother at the small, round wooden table nearest the corner of the kitchen. That old thing was near its breaking point and about to give way. She drank the coffee, shook her head, and loaded it with several more tons of sugar and took a sip.

"Mm, Mm! Now that tastes good."

"Well, I'm glad you got your coffee to your liking, mother." My mother pulled out a chair from the table and sat in it. "What have you come by to insult me on today?"

"I only came to talk to you about the children," Grandmother Helen answered.

From her expression, the coffee seemed delightful that time. While she sat at the table, she began telling a story of how my mother was seventeen and had miraculously walked across the stage with Lawrence on her hip in one hand and her high school diploma in the other. From then on, she didn't know why my mother hadn't done anything productive career-wise.

Grandmother Helen said that despite my mother's grave mistakes at getting pregnant at such an unpropitious time, she was still jubilant to see her youngest daughter walk the stage. She stressed to my mother that she needed to move someplace where I could have my own bedroom instead of cramming me up in small spaces with a boy.

"Now, you know it's not right, Evelyn."

As the discussion heated, my mother only looked at Grandmother Helen as someone who often complained about every little thing she did.

"I can only do what my income allows, mother. If you're so worried about how she's sleeping at night, then how about you buy me a house or give me some money for the kids."

"Well, don't I already?"

"Alright, mother, is there anything else you'd like to insult me further about?"

Grandmother Helen always found herself picking up the pieces and pitching in a few times to help, simply because she hated to see anybody struggling to get by, her daughter most of all. "I have nothing else to say."

She unzipped her purse and removed a few crumpled hundred dollar bills and placed them in the middle of the table and kissed Lawrence and me goodbye. I hated to see her leave so soon, but anytime they argued, she knew it was best to leave my mother to settle down alone. My mother wanted her to leave anyway because she'd been seeing someone after our father left us for a woman named Claire Langston. Our father had been a bag sacker at the local food mart, nearing promotion until he resigned. He was now living the fast life of the streets. He'd fallen head over heels for Claire, and word spread fast that they were getting married soon. My gut told me earlier that there had to be a new man in my mother's life from the way she started carrying herself. From my guess, the mystery man had to be the maintenance guy, and I was correct.

CHAPTER TWO
A NEW ENVIRONMENT

A year passed, and I'd just celebrated my eighth birthday two days before we arrived at our new house on Cotton Bayou. I was breathing in freedom with my mother and her new husband, Victor, the maintenance man from our old apartment. The house was situated atop a steep hill with three well-proportioned bedrooms and one bathroom. It wasn't in the best neck of the woods, but a big step up from our last. It was a new experience for Lawrence and me moving into a house.

A warm cozy feel swept across my shoulders, almost as if it were welcoming me on in. I took a step in and walked towards the back, noticing that finally, I had my own room. That would mean privacy away from my brother. Lawrence and I were each given new beds from Victor. Lawrence had a much bigger bed since he was the oldest. I was thankful to have a roof shading my head overall.

"I'm going out back."

"Alright, don't get into anything you aren't supposed to," my mother said, helping Victor unpack some of the boxes they'd brought in.

I walked out towards the back and realized it was gated. There was an old Amish porch swing not far from a shed that could've belonged to the previous owner. I took a seat in it, and the sound of creaking traveled through my ears as I closed my eyes shut. Softly, I inhaled, then exhaled. When I opened my eyes, that scintillating sun had shone right on them. Through the clouds, it looked like the waves of the ocean. I placed a couple of sunflower seeds on my tongue that Grandmother Helen usually bought me at the local food mart whenever I went along with her, which left a funny but salty taste in my mouth. I twirled in circles with my head held to the sky in the hot summery weather that became too much to bear. The smile upon my face was unbreakable.

My mother yelled for me from the screen door at the back of the house, "Come on in and freshen up! Your father and I also want to talk to you."

I ran to her command, removing my mud-covered shoes first. When I got inside, I noticed a plate full of freshly made golden brown chocolate chip cookies on the table. Gooey chocolate oozed from the middle, crispy edges that left me totally flabbergasted.

"Do you mean our stepfather?" I asked. I took a bite out of one of the cookies and drank from the glass of milk she'd poured.

She looked at me, angrily disgusted with my question. "From now on, Victor is your father. The man you think is your father isn't nothing but a lazy deadbeat that doesn't do anything for you. He doesn't even call unless he feels like it."

I could tell from most things my mother said that she still held a grudge against him. Anyone could see it. She disagreed, saying she forgave him for what he did to her and that she didn't really harbor any bad feelings. I never thought that Victor, forty-five, who had been married once before for years with children, would marry again to someone twenty-seven years his junior.

"You smell funky, Tamara, and you're muddy. Why have you been outside playing around in all that dirt like a boy?"

I looked down and shrugged. "It's not that much, just a little, Mama."

"That's more than just a little dirt. You're covered in so much filth that you don't even look like yourself. Such a nasty and ugly little girl!" She pointed up the staircase that led to the bathroom. "Go bathe yourself right away!"

After I'd gotten out of the tub, I walked to Lawrence's room and opened his door to see him quickly opening a box that contained his PlayStation console. It had been a gift from Victor as well as the new television. He was filled with such exuberance, enough to test out his new video game on it. Victor walked in by surprise and smiled. "So, how do you like everything, Son?"

Lawrence's facial expression went blank, and he looked at Victor for a split second, then turned away, continuing with opening the box. He didn't care for Victor and still missed our father. He'd finally removed the gaming console from the box, and, in his haste, he plugged it into the television.

"I believe I asked a simple question?"

"You already know the answer, so I don't know why you're asking."

"Alright," said Victor, trying to keep his frustration at ease. "I'll just take that as a thank you. Next time, I advise you to watch the words that come from your mouth." Victor walked away, pulling the door up behind him.

Lawrence sat down beside me and began to pout. "I hate that man. Why did our mother have to get married? She has us."

"I don't know. He makes her happy, though. Besides, look at all this stuff he's gotten us." I picked up one of Lawrence's video games and held it up to his face. "See, he's done things for us that our father wouldn't in a million years."

"That doesn't mean anything, yo'."

"Then how come we've barely had anything to play with at our old place? Huh?"

Lawrence and I took a stride over to my new bedroom, decorated with pink & lightly colored purple walls, curtains and a full-sized bed. I flung myself down on the bed. It was much more comfortable to my skin and not as rough on my back as the bed I had. Without hesitation, I was already testing the fluffy yet firm pillows on top. I happily bounced up and down on the bed, and after Lawrence saw how overjoyed I'd been in the moment, he joined in, and we began to pillow fight.

My mother walked in, shocked by what she witnessed.

"Get your asses down from there! What do you think this is? Tamara, you'd better finish unboxing those clothes over yonder."

I said nothing but did as I was told, knowing how she could become.

"Did you hear what I said, little girl?"

"I am, Mama. I'm just trying to straighten my pillows first."

My mother dropped the folded laundry she'd been carrying. She smacked my face, and from how hard she'd delivered the blow, she knocked me back, and I sailed towards a plastic ninja turtle toy chest behind me, missing it by an inch, and I hit the ground. I cried tears of pain as I laid there. I knew better than to look her way or stare into her eyes, or else she would hit me harder than the first time. The more she screamed at me, the more frightened I became. I sniffed back the snot running from my nose and tried wiping my tears. She bent down in rage and spit flung from her tongue, covering my face as she yelled at me once again and pinched my arm until it bled.

"Mama, please, I'm sorry. I'll do what you say from now on."

She looked down on me and responded, "That's what they all say."

I knew my mother didn't play any games when she got on us about things. This time was different, and I didn't know why she'd lashed out in the way she did. She began to twist my arm much worse. I could see that there was no trust; she didn't believe a word that came from my mouth.

Victor walked in. "What's going on in here?"

My mother suddenly let go of my arm. I was hoping that he'd come to save me, put an end to the wretchedness. She looked over at Victor, her face red and inflamed with his intrusion. I could tell she was mostly embarrassed with Victor having to see this side of her.

She turned her attention to me, eyes blazing with indignation as if I'd wronged her, then she thrust me back.

"The next time I tell you to do something, you'd better do it right then."

I nodded apologetically on bended knees. "Yes, mama."

My mother picked up the laundry and walked out of my bedroom, and I looked up at Victor, weeping and broken-hearted that he hadn't done anything. He stared back at me for a minute, then followed my mother. *Who was she?* I have no recollection of my mother ever being sweet to be honest. This was just something far worse. I didn't remember anything fun that just the two of us did together like other mothers I'd seen taking time with their daughters.

Since the marriage, my mother's beauty hadn't been the same. It was like watching the queen in Snow White staring blindly into a mirror, unsatisfied with who she was. She changed herself for Victor, and she had for my father as well. She did everything Victor asked of her, one being to make sure we addressed him as Dad and nothing else. We had better learn to start calling him Dad, or else it would be an automatic punishment. We didn't feel comfortable being forced to call Victor Dad, and neither did my Grandmother Cara, our father's mother, who told people she found it slightly worrying. I had been happy to see her knocking on the door after so long. She told my mother she would stop by to see us for a while, and she had lived up to that.

* * *

"Hi Ev,' I'm here to see the children. First, may I have a word with you?"

I wish she hadn't done that. Anytime she pulled my mother to the side, it was never good. They usually ended up fighting, and if it were over us, I knew how mad my mother would get, especially if she found out I'd told her what she and Victor were making us do.

"What do you want, Cara? If this involves your son, then I don't want any part of it."

Grandmother Cara waved her hand in the air. "Stop it! I'm not here to talk about him. This is about the children. Don't you think it's a bit too much to force the children to call your new husband, Dad?"

My mother looked back at me, eyebrows forming a v-shape as she frowned. That look often made me grow silent and petrified.

"Don't worry about what's going on in my house." She opened the door. "You can let yourself out."

"But Ev,' I came to see my grandchildren. Are you going to deny me that because of what I asked you?"

"You can see them another time."

My mother slammed the door in my Grandmother Cara's face. My emotions were running rampant, and I waited for her to approach me. She reached for my arm and took me off to my room, where I was thrown to the floor. I wanted her to go ahead and do what she had to. What I thought felt like home quickly no longer felt like it anymore. Turmoil was sure to rise between the four of us. What led her to change on me? Was it the men that surfaced in and out of her life before Victor? Or was it something about me she hated?

CHAPTER THREE
BEFORE VICTOR

I can still remember when the candlelit cinnamon aroma overwhelmed the apartment. That night when I hastily ran down the hall to see the devastating look on my mother's face, I peered the corners of her bedroom to see her being thrown to her waterbed. Those were in style, and everybody seemed to want one at the time. She had been rubbing her left cheekbone. My father stood over her fiercely, wearing a blue and white bandana around his head, a heavy silver chain with matching attire that gave off a thuggish appearance. His sandy brown hair, dark blonde Van Dyke beard, skin the color of a cigar with his broad, muscular physique made him appear rather attractive to women.

That night, he'd been sweating profusely. Beneath his brow contained eyes so cold, they screamed sinister. His finger pointed downward, his demands at her throat like a knife slicing right through as she jumped back with tears filling her eyes after she found out he was having another affair.

What's going on in there? I thought.

I had to take a closer look, and I wondered, *had he hit my mother?* I never knew my father to be the abusive type and not to her, though I could see that their relationship had spiraled out of control a year before he left. However, I soon learned that side existed in him.

My father stopped and looked us in the eye along the way after packing the rest of his belongings. He then pushed me to the side and continued heading toward the front door, clutching a designer leather bag in hand. We were saddened to see him leave, not knowing if he would ever return.. We held tightly to each other's hands while we watched him walk out. I suddenly freed my hand from Lawrence's and peeked out the door to see Claire waiting on the passenger side of the car, her hand held up, flashing a princess-cut, white gold diamond ring that put sparkles in her eyes.

"Come back in," said Lawrence, taking me under his arm.

I walked back inside and glanced at my mother, laying in a bed of tears. My only concern was for her. Her whimpers were like that of a puppy, lying down after being wounded.

"Mama, are you okay?"

She sat up in a beautiful red gown. Her eyes were barely open, and they looked like flowers that had been overwatered. Her body was like something that had been shot with an infectious arrow.

"I'm okay. Go on back to your room now, just...just go on, you hear?"

"Mama, where did Daddy go? Is he ever coming back?"

She looked at me, puzzled, tears still hugging her jawbone. "I don't know, and for his good, I hope he never comes back! Go to your room!"

I wasted no time and ran straight to my room. My mother was ultimately shattered, and this left Victor, just four months after to pick up the pieces. She had suffered so much abuse in the past at the hands of our father that Victor could sense it and had no issues in carrying a lot of her baggage. This was a woman Victor knew he truly loved and wanted to marry.

Before they married, she loved leaving delectable box-made desserts at the office for him to pick up after his shift and during his lunch hours. My mother had put away her sorrows, tidied herself and the three of us, and walked down to the office of the complex where Miss Arnette, the landlady, sat with her office assistant.

I heard her as she leaned over and whispered, "Oh, Lord, here she comes again."

"Good morning, Miss Arnette, could you kindly make sure Victor gets these? They are his favorite. I know he would be excited that I brought them over."

My mother handed the container full of goodies to Miss Arnette. I looked up to see a happy and content woman. A huge smile that crossed her face showed it all.

"Sure, Evelyn, what's in here?"

"Oh, those are my famous chocolate pecan brownies. I know that Victor loves pecans."

"Yes, he does. I'll make sure he gets them."

She scanned the clear container full of brownies, and from the face she made, I could tell it was one of a jaded appetite.

"I also put in a maintenance request, so please have him stop by later for me. No one else."

Miss Arnette took sight of my mother joyously swaying her hips and stared grimly at her.

* * *

Victor made a visit to our unit to fix the toilet that flooded our only bathroom after my mother couldn't find the source of the issue. Upon my mother inviting him in, I took note of his medium stature and the dense jerry curl juice running slowly down the nape of his neck. I wanted to tell Victor badly to ease up on the relaxer, even though my mother seemed pleased with the way he was. His shirt was slightly open with visible wool-like chest hair, and dark brown snakeskin boots. We had to put aside our feelings about Victor because either way, our mother wouldn't hear it.

She soon learned that a curious Lawrence had flushed one of his G.I. Joe figures down the drain. After he finished up, it was like love at first sight for them. They couldn't get enough of each other and did anything they could, even within Victor's working hours, to see one another. He lusted after her and showered my mother with the finer things that our father refused to do. He always showed up late at night with flowers when they thought Lawrence and I were sound asleep.

I knew there was nothing that needed fixing at that hour except for her, I guess. They sat down in the living room, laughing and talking fondly of one another on that smooth, black and burgundy loveseat she always loved. They locked eyes like lovers lost in paradise. I peeked in to see him rubbing her soft cheeks in a circular motion, brushing his puckered lips against hers. Mother always loved the feel of that couch, so it made the moment even more intense for them. I could tell that whatever Victor was doing, she enjoyed it from the loud giggles and the way she pulled him closer to her.

I rolled my eyes at the sight of them kissing. "Yuck!"

My mother yelled, "Tamara is that you? If it is, you'd better get your behind in that bed!"

I darted back to my bedroom, lying there hearing those voices of love travel the halls into the room that Lawrence and I slept in at the time. I was happy to see that my mother had found love again in someone she truly trusted. Though I was happy for her, I was afraid of the new man entering her life. It would be a change, not just for her but for us. Victor knew how to talk a good game, and many others who knew him also said he had a way with the ladies back in the day. I could tell that he did from the way he'd already swooped in and stolen my mother's heart so easily from the very first day.

It doesn't take much with your mother anyway. She's easy. That's what my father used to imply.

He always said disrespectful things about her that young children shouldn't have to hear coming from the other parent's mouth. Victor, on the other hand, manifested kindness when it came to her but held a benevolent smile when he visited. He was almost always communicative with everyone around him, easily liked by people that barely knew him around Monroe, though my family didn't take much liking to him.

CHAPTER FOUR

1992

I immediately woke from a horrible nightmare drenched in sweat, drained and dehydrated. The nightmare had been about the day my father walked out without saying goodbye. My mother always suffered a high level of stress with the way our father mistreated her, so she took a vow never to let anyone get between her and Victor. I didn't blame my mother for feeling that way, but I did blame her for not listening to my feelings. Mostly, for placing every man before us when the love should've been equally divided. I didn't expect her to make me the highest priority over her marriage because that could potentially damage what she and Victor had going on. However, I did expect genuine love in return.

Furthermore, I needed her understanding of things. She was too busy with Victor at times to give me the motherly attention I sought.

Somehow, she never seemed to lack that with Lawrence. She comforted Lawrence in a time of need and told him she loved him. She became so emotionally unavailable to me that it punctured my heart. I walked into the living room after washing my face and brushing my teeth and saw my mother, who seemed ready to jump down my neck about something.

"Tamara, get these damn toys off the floor. What do you think this is, a daycare?"

She kicked a few of my toys to the left side of the den area and waited for my response.

"No, ma'am."

"Well, then, get this mess picked up before your father gets home."

"He's not our father," Lawrence rudely interrupted. He had no problems making the ill feelings he had for Victor known.

"Son, please, I don't have time for this today." She took a few dollars from her pocket, then placed her hand on his shoulder. "Here's a few dollars. Go to the corner store with your friends or go play. I'm talking to your sister right now."

"Yeah, alright, but that old man still isn't our father."

Lawrence walked away, and I hurriedly gathered the remainder of the toys from the floor before my mother could look my way.

"You thought that was funny with your fast ass, didn't you?"

"No, I didn't laugh. I was picking up the rest of my things as you told me to do."

She snatched the toys from my hand and yanked me by my ponytail until my head couldn't go back any further. She blabbered on for ten good minutes of how evil I was and how I was the devil's child.

"Stop, Mama! That hurts."

"Shut up! Do you know what happens to disobedient children like you?"

She pounded my face violently against her fist and used the car keys that were lying nearby as a weapon against me.

"I brought you into this world. I can take you right back out," she said.

My mother forcefully threw the car keys at the side of my forehead, cutting me and shouting that I was nothing more than a mistake she wished she could take back. It was hurtful to hear those words, and my head burned as I touched the wound on my forehead and held out my finger, taking note of the bright red blood over my index finger. She hollered for me to pick up the toys, and though I was outraged to see them kicked and scattered over the floor, I said nothing and put them back in the toy bucket where they belonged.

"Sometimes, I wonder about you and what's going on in that head of yours. I know that you've been talking about me behind my back when I'm not around. Haven't you? That's just what the devil does."

My mother was religious and believed in a lot of things that Victor had. It hadn't been until she met him when she began to attend church. How she went about the word of the Bible had been the total opposite of what our church pastor spoke on Sundays. She and Victor constantly anointed the house with oil. They said it was the best way to keep things calm with everything that went on in our home. Every fight my mother and I got into had given me bad nightmares, triggering past traumas of the night when Uncle Mike, my mother's youngest brother, was killed by drug dealers.

Uncle Mike was very sweet and kind to Lawrence and I. However, he was careless and the type of person who stayed in trouble with the law. He liked getting his fingers sticky whenever he could with his drug-addicted buddies. They were always up to no good, dozing off on my mother's couch, high on methamphetamine, while she was away. He did my mother lots of favors, but there was one night when all hell took over in our apartment. Intruders broke in, valuables were stolen, and the place was trashed. Lawrence picked me up in his arms and did the best that he could to shield me with our mother's clothes. He pulled each one off the hangers, and they came tumbling down on top of me, where we hid underneath. The chaos continued in the front room. The intruders knocked over every piece of furniture in their path to teach Uncle Mike a lesson. We were lucky to still be alive, Uncle Mike, unfortunately, succumbed to his injuries. Rehab had never done him any good. My mother knew this, but she still left us in his care while she went out on the town with her girlfriends. The negative things my father said to me were beginning to shine some light. It was as if I, most of all, had ruined her life. No child really asks to be here, but most of us are thankful that we are anyway.

"What's all that noise?"

My mother ran into my bedroom, observing it from wall to closet.

"Nothing, Mama, I was having a bad nightmare, I think."

"That's what happens when you're bad and eat sugar before bed. It was nothing but the devil attacking you. Lay on back down."

The very next morning, I woke for breakfast but not before washing up, and I knew that I'd better have my behind at the table on time. If I didn't like what she cooked, then I went without eating. I took a seat at the table, waiting for my plate to be put before me.

"So, you think you can tell people what's going on in this house?"

Her eyes flickered, and in them, I could see a woman enraged, storming in my direction. I didn't have the slightest hint of what she was talking about. I just waited for her to strike me as usual.

"No, Mama, I... I-" I tried to catch my breath and took a minute to swallow. "I didn't tell anyone anything."

The only thing I remembered saying was that she and Victor were making us call him Dad. There was nothing else that I could think of. Before I could speak another word, I was knocked hard against the large oak armoire behind me.

"You little witch, I should knock the living daylights out of you right now. You're lucky I'm not in the mood. The only reason you're still standing is that I'm allowing you too," stated my mother.

This woman was supposed to be my mother, and she was acting more like a bully exposed in her true form. Lawrence, well, he could do no wrong. He was her baby boy, so I took the blame for everything with a harsher sentence.

My family mostly valued and favored boys more than they did the girls. If you were a girl in the family who they happened to like well, then consider it as a blessing or luck, for the most part. Every negative thing my mother said had outweighed the good and was imprinted on my heart.

CHAPTER FIVE

Where Were You When I Needed You?

It had been a Thursday morning, and what seemed the beginning of a rainy and dreary season. This was the second time when I'd been dropped off in Victor's minivan by my mother. The minivan had a few missing windows, each side covered with plastic bags. I used to beg her to stop at the end of the corner to drop me off, to let me walk the rest of the way like Victor had. Instead, she was bent on embarrassing me and dropped me off in front of the school building. He'd just taught her how to drive because she never knew how. We always caught the bus.

I ran in as fast as my feet would let me to get to class before the bell rang but was stopped by someone shouting behind me.

"Stop your running, young lady, before you fall."

It was the grumpy old brood of fourth grade, Ms. Vastwell, whose glasses always hung down to almost the tip of her nose. She would adjust those wide bifocals to her eyebrows which drew inward before she approached you. She loved shouting at anyone who passed her and thought she was the boss of just about everyone. It was better to find another way around Ms. Vastwell if you could. Even the staff of the school disliked and avoided Ms. Vastwell.

"Sorry, Ms. Vastwell, I'm trying not to be late for class."

"Then you should learn to get to school much earlier than you do. Be on your way now and slow it down a little."

She gestured me toward the side double doors, pointing her ruler and almost hitting me with it. I ducked and hurried to class.

The bell rung again, and I knew that I was late—three minutes past the normal. I had been tardy for class before.

Dang, what am I going to tell the teacher now?

My mother told me that I needed to make sure that I got to class on time, even though she had been the one dropping me off too close to the start time. She blamed me for getting dressed too slow when I was already up in the mornings, bright and bushy, waiting by the door for her.

"I see you're late again," said Mrs. Bradley.

Mrs. Bradley might have been a favorite schoolteacher of mine, but she kept track of each of her students more than any other teachers and got on us when we weren't doing well.

"Yes, but I swear I tried to get to class on time."

"And why didn't you?"

I was so afraid to tell her that it was my mother's fault that I had been that late. Arriving at 7:19 a.m. To make things better for myself, I told her that I made a trip by the little girls' room first.

"Now, Tamara, you know the rules, procedures, and consequences of the class, don't you?"

"Yes, ma'am."

"And what are they?"

"That all students must take care of his or her personal business before the bell rings unless told otherwise."

"That is correct, but that isn't everything. I'm going to let what you did slide this time. Do not keep doing this up, or I will have to contact your mother."

When she said that, I instantly felt under pressure and slowly walked to my desk, moving with a shuddering twitchiness, and I began to bite my nails.

"You used to have perfect attendance in my class," Mrs. Bradley yelled from across the room.

"Lately, you haven't been very focused, young lady."

She went back to the chalkboard to begin her morning lecture. My head lowered to my scrawny little legs, body rocking stormily back and forth in my chair, where I mumbled to myself, "She can't! No, she mustn't tell my mother!"

I began to have an indescribable feeling in my bones. The kind that tingles nervously throughout your bones so much that you can't control it. The classroom looked as if it were being stretched and spaced out before me. The left side of my head began to ache badly like cluster headaches attacking me. It caused me to let out a great deal of pain. One of my classmates took a gander at my pants as I sat down and looked at me funny and asked if I were okay. I wasn't, but I didn't know how to say it.

I looked down to see that I had wet myself. Without any further thoughts, I scampered up and out of the classroom from everyone. I didn't want anyone to notice and run the risk of being humiliated. Mrs. Bradley rushed after me and realized the accident I had and sent me to nurse Randi's station, where I could get a pair of fresh clothing and underwear to wear while I waited for them to call my mother. I also began vomiting. This wasn't good, taking my mother away from the things she told me she had to do. She would be furious. What other choice did I really have anyway?

The room where I waited was quite colorful, rainbow-colored and eye-catching. The soft, adorable cushioned teddy bears that were stacked neatly against the wall caught my attention. Before I could grab one, my mother stormed in through the door of the activity center.

"Let's go now! Come on, get up!"

"I'm sorry, Mama."

Nothing I said ever mattered. She marched me to the visitor's side of the parking lot, where her best friend Alondria sat waiting on her. My mother pinched me until my arm turned strawberry red and then took me by that same arm and tossed me in the backseat of the car. Alondria frowned confusedly and rolled her eyes at me from the rearview mirror.

I never saw it coming, but my mother reached from the front seat, throwing several blows that I tried my hardest to block with what little strength I had. I sheltered my face mostly from her. It seemed to be what she had been going for the most.

Alondria was right behind her, yelling, "You're too old to still be wetting yourself. You need to grow up!"

I could sense that from the whole ride home, anger was building. My mother couldn't wait to get me home to tear one into my behind.

She did just that, whacking me over the head and tearing into me with the switch Victor had given her to keep in the laundry room area if

Lawrence and I got out of place. My mother grabbed me by my throat and called me the devil's spawn. I could feel my life slowly slipping away until she finally loosened her grip. Over time, several more whippings had been introduced. I longed for a man, my father, who never saved me. In times that I found myself alone, I asked God, where was he? Why would he let me suffer?

It was an environment I didn't want to live a life in anymore. Though I needed my mother like every other daughter and wanted to share with her how I really felt, I was afraid of her, petrified to speak up. I knew if I did, she would disagree with every word, and worse, I'd suffer more beatings. I secretly called my father during the night, knowing I wasn't allowed to use the landline phone. Surprisingly, my father answered; sadly, he wasn't happy to hear from me and never stayed on the phone long. Only a few words were exchanged. He never understood my pain, and neither did she. They saw what they wanted to see and what they wanted to believe, not what was happening to me.

CHAPTER SIX
BATTERED AND BRUISED

I had been outside in the back yard of Grandmother Helen's, mid-July, playing and enjoying the cool refreshing weather that in short periods interrupted the rising temperatures of the sun. I decided to take shade from the oppressive summer heat and slumped down in a lawn chair to take a nap. It had been so relaxing until it was cut short by the sound of Victor's guttural accent.

"Is your mother in the house, or is she out back?"

Lawrence responded, "I don't know. What do you think?"

Lawrence's attitude had become alarming. I looked over to where Victor stood, his face outraged at the response he had delivered. Victor snarled up at him in frustration.

"Look, I know I'm not your biological father, but you will not continue to live under my roof and disrespect me. When I ask you a question, answer me properly."

"And I'm not your son. Never will be, so why don't you stop calling me that."

I knew that Lawrence was just as hurt as I was from everything that had been going on, but I couldn't believe the words he said sometimes. It caused an even bigger argument between them. Victor stepped close to Lawrence and looked him directly in his eyes as though he were approaching him to sucker punch him. Lawrence stood boldly, waiting on Victor's next moves. Lawrence's best friend Ardell, who only lived a few blocks away, was the lifesaver of it all after he ran up and yelled out Lawrence's name, breaking the eye competition between them. I knew it wasn't easy for Victor to take us in and deal with the attitude issues Lawrence presented each time. It was a commitment that he knew he made when he married our mother.

Everyone settled in around the kitchen table, smiling and passing around fine china to one another. Lawrence was nowhere in sight, so I figured he must've still been outside and angry with Victor. I excused myself from the dinner table. My mother shouted for me to hurry back.

I discovered him in the same spot he'd been in earlier. "You know you can't keep making Victor mad. He doesn't like that."

Lawrence's face held a disgruntled look. "Forget that old man. He can't tell me what to do."

I decided it was best to leave him to some time to himself. Maybe then he'd cool down before coming inside. Grandmother Helen worried about Lawrence. He had always been her favorite grandson. She came running toward Lawrence just as I opened the door to let myself back in.

"Why don't you come on in with the family to eat! It's getting late, and you shouldn't be out with these mosquitos unless you want to get eaten up, ya' hear?"

"I'll come in when I'm ready," Lawrence stated.

"Boy, don't you hear your grandmother talking to you?" It was Victor. This time, he was very upset by the disrespect displayed by Lawrence. Victor's voice was tumultuous that time, as he backed my Grandmother in her argument. She didn't like Victor and wasn't very accepting of any of my mother's former boyfriends either, except our father, who had a way of easily charming people like my family in. All it had been was a web of manipulation, and it had taken effect alright.

Grandmother Helen decided to quiet herself while Victor stood next to her, studying Lawrence and taking notes for what he should do to him later. She had an odd feeling about Victor when it came to her grandson; no one was really allowed to touch him, but on this subject, she couldn't have agreed more that Lawrence needed to obey.

"Under whose orders? You aren't my daddy," said Lawrence.

I decided to be little Miss Nosy and walked out for a better view of things. I could see that Victor's eyes had met my brother's as if they were having a stare off competition yet again. It was obvious that he was fed up with Lawrence's bickering. My mother came out and was able to get them both inside, and everyone gathered in the living room, all but Lawrence, who disappeared. Everyone's stomachs were full, rubbing their stuffed bellies with great pleasure, while I sat at the table still feasting. Suddenly, I was caught off guard by Lawrence, rushing in like something was terribly wrong. He wore only a t-shirt and drawers.

"I have a surprise to show you."

Lawrence held out lots of balled up tissue rolled in one hand and uncovered it under Victor's nose. Something brown and icky was on top, human feces.

"Here, smell my shit! You deserve it. It's your special Thanksgiving meal!"

It seemed to be hysterically funny to Lawrence. Everybody was in disbelief, and the room had grown silent. Victor was mortified after all he'd done for Lawrence to be disrespected in such a manner. I couldn't believe what he had done. It was clear he truly disliked him.

Victor stood up and demanded that my mother quickly round up our things to prepare to leave.

"Tamara, let's go! Whatever you haven't eaten, just take it with you."

The flames burning in Victor's eyes told many stories. Mostly around my Grandmother Helen,

I could tell he tried to keep a cool and calm composure. I kissed her goodbye. She looked back at me worried, then turned to Lawrence, disappointed. She hugged him, then tried shaking some sense into him. "Boy, you know better than what you did. That was inhumane."

We got in the car, and Lawrence began taunting Victor with the smirk that crossed his face. He slammed the vehicle door behind us while my mother tried to convince him to calm down. It was no use. Victor could barely maintain his anger. He sped home senselessly, and my mother kept her face turned toward the window, praying and holding on tightly to her seatbelt for dear life that she'd make it home in one piece. I could see that her face had turned pale and that she was just as shocked as I was by Lawrence's behavior. She feared for him.

Victor told Lawrence to strip down to nothing but his underwear. His voice roared throughout the room in a deep, loud, and heavy toned voice, like an alpha lion at the neck of his prey. Lawrence was panic-stricken, and fear had already set in. I had become afraid myself. I wanted to take off, but something inside me needed to stay around to watch. I wanted to see what he'd do to my brother, who I worried so much about. I knew that Victor was a strict man whose bark was louder than his bite. He wanted things done a certain way with us, but this seemed like a night of no other, and one that the both of us would always have as a childhood memory.

"No, I will not!"

Victor stepped up to Lawrence and responded, "So, many times, you've back-talked me and told me what you weren't going to do." Victor shook his head and stepped closer, invading Lawrence's personal space. "Well, I'll teach you a lesson."

Screams poured throughout the house. I covered my ears, watching my stepfather violently whip Lawrence across his back, legs, arms, and chest with several switches tied together with thick rubber bands and long pointy thorns. I could see his flesh. Victor said the switches were handpicked specifically for Lawrence. He tried desperately to run away from Victor, but he followed right behind in fury, finding him behind the sofa in the den area.

"I'm sorry!" Lawrence cried.

He saw that hiding and apologizing made no difference because Victor was angry, and he always found him. He rushed in like a madman, creating deeper welts from the flex rods that covered his body even more than it had before.

"That's enough!" I screamed at Victor, who ignored my demands.

"You better shut your mouth before you find yourself next!" my mother shouted angrily.

She sat nearby, arms folded, nose tilted to the ceiling. She was a woman who stood by her every word, so I made sure that I kept quiet. She watched as the whippings continued and never once tried to intervene, side-eyeing me, yelling, "It's all your fault!"

I really didn't know how that was true when Lawrence was the one who ticked Victor off.

I felt she shouldn't have let it go that far or the way that it did. I watched helplessly, seeing the blood pour from Lawrence's body. He begged and pleaded with Victor for mercy, but still, the whippings continued.

"Dad, please, I'm bleeding."

"So, now you call me, Dad? It would have helped if you had thought about that before, so I could care less about you bleeding. You need this butt whipping."

The flex rod tore through his underwear to his skin, leaving deep open wounds of his bare bottom visible. This not only put more fear in my eyes but into Lawrence's. We didn't know what Victor might do if we did something else wrong, but we would make sure to avoid any wrongdoings from now on, even the smallest things.

After the whipping ended, I waited until Victor exited the room to slide next to my very wounded brother on the floor. He balled up like an infant cradling itself and sobbed uncontrollably. At that instance, I wanted to yell for help, but who would hear me besides my mother and Victor? Our father only came around when he felt like it, so I couldn't call him. I wondered if he'd care. Since he had a new wife and life he cherished so much, why would I bother now? I felt like the big sister in this moment, taking care of her older brother when I tended to his wounds.

I tried not to cause any more pain than he had already endured, so I decided to use peroxide rather than alcohol on his open wounds.

"No, it will burn!"

"Lawrence, you have to let me, or your wounds won't heal properly."

"I don't care. I just want to go to sleep. I miss our dad, don't you?"

"Sometimes, I do. He isn't here, so we just must obey. I know you don't want to walk around school looking like this, do you?"

"Well, I should, maybe then we'll get taken away from this horrible hell hole."

I felt sorry for him, even though he had disrespected Victor, the punishment could have been much different.

"I think it's right to tell someone, but we could get put in a foster home, Lawrence. Worse, split from each other. What would we do then?"

"Yeah, I guess you've got a point, little sis."

I continued to gently apply the peroxide to his wounds while he laid in my lap resting peacefully.

CHAPTER SEVEN

ENVIOUS

The next day, my mother rushed to me, and I felt a smack come down hard on my right jawbone.

"You think you're all that, huh? Bouncing your little tail in front of my husband."

A few years had gone by, and I was ten years old, but I had no idea what she'd been talking about.

I looked back at her, one eyebrow raised slightly higher than the other, swallowing several times before I could find the right words to form and responded, "No, I never did that!"

I took as many steps back as quickly as I could. The things she accused me of were unbelievable. I didn't know why she did them, but maybe it was to finally get me sent far away, someplace where she didn't have to deal with the likes of me anymore.

"Are you calling me a liar? You wouldn't look half as decent as you do if it weren't for me, do you know that?"

I was taught to respect my elders, but there's a limit to children as well. No child deserves abuse and disrespect from their parents, who, most times, become their child's first bully. Things had gotten out of hand. My jaw felt like she had taken a hammer and shattered it. To my surprise, I could see her hand rising towards the sky and coming down fast to strike me. I tried my best to dodge her and hid between the gaps of Victor's old work desk.

"Stop it!" I yelled, my body sore and tired from being used as her punching bag."

"Get over here, you witch!"

She pulled me from under the desk, and I knew that it was better that I just take it rather than run. It would only add on to the punishment, she would say.

She opened her closet door and took out one of her worn-out red stilettos and began pounding into me. It left a long scar running along my back, and when I tried to defend myself, my hand had been caught and cut by the ends of her sharp heel. It was going to be a scar that would remain there forever, and I'd always remember where and who it came from. If that didn't anger her enough, then defending myself from being thrown out the house surely did.

"Get out! Get out of my house, witch!"

"Mother, please, where will I go?"

She yelled, "Quite frankly, I wouldn't give a damn where you went as long as you aren't here anymore!"

She packed my belongings and tossed them outside right along with me. Our relationship was strained. We didn't see eye to eye on much of anything. I never knew why my mother hated me so much. I tried to do everything I could to reconcile the matter, but how much could a ten-year-old say to get her mother to listen when she still didn't have a care in the world or acted paranoid for the most part?

"What did I do wrong, Mama?"

Not a word was spoken. I looked down to see she had ripped my favorite Aaliyah shirt in two, the late singer, who I had always idolized. The scarring of my kneecaps had taken on a purple and blackish color, and the pain was even more intense than before. I rubbed my top lip next to what felt like a huge bump and cried out in pain. I felt impaled with no perception of complacency or confidence anymore. The harder I tried to keep from being thrown out of the house, frantic from what she might do next, the angrier she became. She wouldn't have it. My tiny body was no match against her, so she took the steps of slamming my foot in the door a couple of times until I fell back. My mother was triumphant. I was out of the house, telling myself that everything would be alright, and most of all, change would surely come. I believed that. I yelled at the top of my lungs in so much pain, seeing the blood shoot out from my big toe, causing more excruciating pain.

My foot bled through the brand-new clear jellybean sandal that my grandmother Cara had given me two weeks prior. I was stuck outside, hopping around with a bad foot injury and looking for someplace to go. I wasn't prepared for the world outside and what the streets possibly had in store for a girl my age.

I noticed other children playing in their front yards with their mothers and fathers, so no one really took notice of me hopping along the dirty pavement with the small blood trail that followed me.

"Hey girl, are you okay? What are you doing?"

Candice, the only true friend that I had on the block, appeared out of nowhere.

"I'm fine." I crossed one leg behind the other so that she wouldn't notice the blood. "I'm just out here, looking for something."

She attended the same school and walked home with me in the evenings. She was leader of the school's cheer squad that my mother refused to let me be a part of. My mother was always hot under the collar about it, saying that only sluts and fast girls were cheerleaders. I wasn't really allowed to participate in anything at school.

"What's wrong with your foot?"

She had way too many questions that I didn't bother to answer anymore. I pretended not to hear her and walked away. I was in too much pain for any type of conversation. When I looked at my feet, I saw that it had swollen, and my speed had been delayed. I limped until I reached the next street over and felt the little strength that I had disconnecting from my body. I was too ashamed to be around Candice while I was injured, fearing that her mother might call the police on my mother, whom I always tried to protect. She may have hurt me in the worst way possible, but I still had love for her. Rain began to pour. In the meantime, I took shelter under a wide tall tree with broken limbs that resembled my life, broken, some parts barely hanging on. I was happy to be away from that house of horrors.

* * *

The evening faded into the night, and while I sat there sobbing and gazing at the sky surrounded by the beautifully lit stars, I asked God what most people ask all the time. Why me? Why'd you put me here on this earth if you knew I would suffer? I could see the headlights from Victor's minivan speeding into the driveway. From the way he rushed to meet my mother in the yard, he seemed livid about something.

Lawrence ran outside. The next thing I'd noticed was him sauntering down the very same sidewalk I'd been walking down earlier while Victor stayed behind in a quarrel with my mother. I hadn't gone very far from home and had been walking back when I saw Lawrence running in my direction and calling out, "Sis, where are you?"

I was agitated and upset with him, that he'd only come back to watch the fight between my mother and I. He hadn't done or said a thing to help me.

He stopped where he was and rubbed his chin. "Hey, Sis, is that you?"

"Yeah, and what do you want?"

I was more annoyed by his presence because he hadn't been the protector that most brothers are. He wasn't sticking up for me anymore, like he had in the past. He was taking up for my mother or, as they say, a mama's boy. He stood by and watched while I took the severe and unfair beatings from our mother.

"Dad said to come home. Here, let me help you up."

"No! I've got it. Just leave me alone!"

It took us a while to get back home because of my injured foot. I was relieved when we finally made it. Upon entering, my mother had been riled up by an argument she and Victor had been into over me. She stood in the doorway, head tilted to the side, lips curved upwards with a look that told me she wished she'd never brought me into the world. I kept my head lowered and went straight for the bathroom to tend to my injured foot. I stared in the mirror and wasn't happy with what I saw. My mother always did make me feel less pretty in the shade of my own skin. She once told me that I would've looked better and would have been the most beautiful light-skinned child a family could hope for had her high school sweetheart, Michael Ealodt, not died, and she wouldn't have had to bother dealing with our father's drama either. I was satisfied with my caramel complexion. She was color struck and didn't know how to deal with her own insecurities.

SHAD'E ZUIWETA

CHAPTER EIGHT

Torn

I refused to eat an unwholesome dinner Victor had prepared on a late Saturday evening that gave off a revolting smell and decided to stuff the contents into a paper towel where it couldn't be seen. I proceeded to throw them in the garbage bin near the back door when I saw him walking in. I didn't think Victor would look inside the garbage, but he spotted it right away when he'd thrown a filthy napkin away. He was furious to see I'd thrown away perfectly good food, something most people don't have and beg for. As a child, I didn't know any better. I knew I was in deep water, and the guilt-ridden look on my face sold me.

"Sorry about that, Dad, I wasn't hungry."

"So, you think that gave you a right to throw away my hard-earned money, girl?"

My mother entered the kitchen, egging the situation on.

"You should tear a real good one into her behind," she said, rinsing the soap suds from the last few dirty dishes in the sink.

"You heard your mama, get on up!"

I hated living with them. I really did. I snatched back my arm and pulled out a chair to sit down. I had never done that before, only Lawrence. I told Victor that I wouldn't be going anywhere to get the whipping he felt was owed to me. Victor, in a quick and abrupt manner, grabbed me again and swung me from the dinner table, where the chair fell underneath me. I tumbled instantaneously to the ground, scarring my chin and tried to raise my body from the surface of the hardwood flooring, but my right leg started to pain. Victor took my legs and dragged me down the hall area of the house as I desperately clung to the walls, trying to stop him from dragging me down further.

I could hear my mother shouting, punctuated by bursts of static to my ears. It was hard to make out. I felt myself losing grip, my nails chipping one by one. I howled in despair for my mother, but she wouldn't come, and she hadn't come to my rescue for a long time. Everything seemed to be about her, and if things didn't go her way, she would throw a tantrum and with Victor also. I was tossed onto the flat ivory full-size metal bed when Victor began to shout in such hostility.

"You've had this one coming for a while now." He removed his belt from the loops of his jeans. "I'm not going to do you like I did your brother. I'll take it easy on you because you're a girl."

"I'm sorry. Please, I promise I won't throw any more food away."

Fear only grew deeper in my gut. I didn't believe those words for a split-itching second. It was still no telling what was going to happen to me after seeing my brother get the worst whipping of his entire life. The door was cracked.

Lawrence peeked through when Victor noticed him and shut it in his face.

"This is only me chastising you. Believe me when I say you guys will thank me later when you're adults."

All I could feel was my thighs stinging. After it was over, I cradled myself in one of the corners of my bedroom. He didn't whip me as badly as my brother. Victor did stand by that, but the two slashes across my left thigh area were bleeding, and it made me a believer of how serious he was. There was no way out.

Three days later, a loud bang sounded at the door. An unexpected visitor had come, but none of us knew who it was. Victor opened the door, and a woman stood dressed in an all-black dress suit and a name tag labeled *Child Protective Services*. My mother hurried me along to my bedroom to quickly change out of my shorts into a pair of jean capris to cover up the bruises on my thighs. Victor said it had to have been my father's doing why the woman showed, that he'd always been trying to find some dirt on them to have us taken away since they married, even though I had never spoken with my father once. I didn't know why he'd want us if he never reached out.

She talked to Lawrence and me alone in the living room for a good thirty minutes. It was a steamy interrogation that was closed fast and went cold after Lawrence and I refused to tell the social worker the truth. With our parents nearby in the other room, we were afraid we might be taken away from them for good and placed with someone much worse. We vowed not to say a thing. In my heart, something was telling me to speak up then. I didn't need anything negative getting back to my mother hearing a mouthful. I needed to avoid the beatings.

After the woman left, I knew she had been on the phone trying to reach out to my father, who on the speakerphone seemed distressed at her tone when she called. He either hung up in her face or said he would stop by when he got the chance to see me. My mother and I fought more over the night. She packed my things, dressed me in a short little white dress that barely fit me, with dirty ankle eyelet frilly socks, glossy white church shoes, and a pink ribbon to top it off. She dropped me off in front of Lincoln Elementary, stranded with nowhere to go, and kept hauling. My mother told me before she left that she would phone my father to pick me up because, per her words, she was done with me.

* * *

My father drove into the school parking lot and got out of the car suited up nicely. This was unusual from his normal taste in clothing. After getting the devastating news that I had been basically abandoned in front of my school in the middle of the night, he drove to get me. I was cold, shivering from my knees up in a dress and worried a stranger would come along and possibly take me away before he arrived. I didn't want to end up like one of those children I felt sorry for on the back of a milk carton with a before and after picture of what they'd potentially looked like in the present tense. He told me that he would've given me a jacket, but he had none to spare. Most people would lend you the one off their back. He didn't. I was hungry, shivering, and shaking my butt cheeks off in that bitterly cold weather.

He shrugged his shoulders and grabbed my bags. "Wow, your mother is as crazy as I thought, and she dressed you up for me, I see."

He hurried me to the car, where I discovered his wife Claire had been sitting in the front seat smiling. I was missing Lawrence and began worrying about him back at that house of horrors with my mother and Victor. I was going to be living with my father and his new wife now. The whole ride to their home, she had been giggling and making fun of my appearance. I hadn't gotten a warm welcome from Claire at all.

"Dane, gone, girl, you look cute with your little white dress!"

"Well, I would say thank you if I thought you meant that in a good way."

"What did you say?"

I wiped the fog from the window, setting a clear view for me to see through. Streetlights lit up the dark roads, and only a few cars had passed by. I didn't know what to say and took a moment to think before I replied, "I meant thank you."

I disliked Claire, but I knew I couldn't just get in the car and start saying whatever I wanted. What if they were to pull over and throw me out because of it? Would he be that cruel as my mother had?

"So, your mom basically dressed you up like you were on your way to a baptism, then abandoned you. How does that feel?"

My father raised his hand, signaling for her to stop. I'm glad he did. I didn't know how I was going to respond to that question. I wanted badly to give her a big chunk of my mind, but I knew he wouldn't let that happen. I learned quickly that no one could voice their opinion about him or his new bride in a negative light, even if it were true.

We were finally at their place. I hadn't visited it before, but when I stepped inside, all I took in was a gorgeous site—one unlike what my mother and Victor shared. Claire stopped me at the doormat and told me to leave my bags on the porch.

"I will have to check your clothes and your bags." She folded one arm over the other and gave me a long contemplating look before her face curled into a smirk, "knowing where you just came from; you might have roaches in there."

She made the ugliest face and pinched her nose while fanning my duffle bag with her hand. My father told her to make sure she sprayed it down good with Raid; then she was told to bring it to him to be triple checked for anything she might have overlooked. My father was very conceited. He believed that no one or anything was above him, not even God himself; he wanted me to fully understand that, living under his roof. His belief was that his cooking was superior, so he was too good to eat other people's food or from their dishes. Not even Grandmother Cara's dishes had been clean enough for him to eat from. I had to eat his food and love it.

"Tamara, come on in here to the kitchen!" he yelled.

When I walked in, he appeared to have a loathsome grin on his face, a hostile stare that focused upon me. I didn't know why he looked at me like that when he hadn't with the twin boys he shared with Claire. They'd given them the names, Jesse and Jeremiah. It made me feel like an outcast. He said that he needed to ask me some very serious questions, and that it was very important that I not lie but answer them truthfully.

"Is there anything going on between you and Victor?"

I was shocked to hear such a question, but I had dealt with it from my mother, so it wasn't hard to understand what he'd been trying to truly ask.

"Of course not, why would you ask that?"

"Because your mother has accused you of being too close with him. She even says that you've been doing things out of the ordinary around him."

"What? No! What did she mean by me being too close to him?"

"I'm not going to get into all of that right now. From now on, keep a good distance from Victor. Your mother thinks you're doing some inappropriate things around him, even though I know she can be a bit insecure."

"Alright I will, but nothing is going on between Victor and I."

He looked satisfied with the answer I gave him.

"Why would she say that about me?"

I was so hurt that I let my anger get the best of me. I was like an emotional rollercoaster, telling him how I really felt about her, and that she hadn't been a real mother to me. My head was spinning round' and round,' and I couldn't take control.

"Stop it, Tamara. She is doing her best."

"Oh, so you're taking up for her now? How do you know what she's trying to do when you're never there?"

"I suggest you shut your damn mouth!"

The voice he yelled was one I had never heard before. He said that I needed to seriously take a chill pill and go straight to bed. I saw my way out, and the twins came rushing in and jumped into his lap.

"Daddy! Daddy!"

"Oh, come here, you guys." He took both boys into his lap and hugged them tight. "So, what'll it be tonight?"

"Can you read us Green Eggs and Ham by Dr. Seuss?"

The three looked so happy. I had not experienced such love. They playfully wrestled one another on the champagne textured carpet, and I stood there wishing it had been me instead. It hurt terribly to watch them, and I couldn't take it anymore. I ran past Claire, bawling tears. I closed the bedroom door behind me, and as I fell asleep, I had to remember that it is often the deepest pain that empowers us to grow into a higher place. I had to remain strong.

CHAPTER NINE
DIAGNOSIS

I was back into the care of my mother, and my birthday was quickly approaching. It was only one week after that my father told her he needed to focus on his own family for a while. I was steadily counting down the weeks that I knew I'd be getting vast sums of money from either my aunt Kelly, who would be coming in town soon from Austin, Texas or Grandmother Helen for my birthday.

I strutted toward the bar area of the kitchen and launched at the cherry-flavored pop tarts that were hot n' ready, waiting for me on a plate. A hickory smoke aroma filled the kitchen and Victor had been on the other side cooking.

"Dang, you're getting down in here, aren't you?" I asked. I shook my head. You've got to love it when you walk in the kitchen early in the morning and a good breakfast is already there waiting for you.

I sunk my teeth into the pop tarts and soon after Victor walked up to me with an unexpected appetizing breakfast he'd prepared. "Oh, well, you know how I do it. Here's your plate," he said, carefully placing a knife and fork on the table. "Eat up!"

I found it very nice that he'd made me a plate, but I also knew Victor loved it when people sampled his food. He enjoyed cooking over anything else and had been a chef before he went into maintenance. I didn't understand why he left the profession in that case, I guess he wanted to try something new for a change.

"Mmm, it smells so good. Thank you." I picked up a utensil and brought the plate closer to me.

I looked down to see he'd whipped up a nice batch of homemade golden-brown pancakes, melted cheese eggs and crisp applewood bacon. My mother really didn't know how to cook, so

Victor worked and did most of that around the house. He would help me with schoolwork when there was no one else that I could turn to, cooking my favorite foods now, and taking me to the bakery shop after school to get my favorite snacks, even when he claimed to be broke. I like how he seemed to have come around.

I looked at Victor. His eyes were bloodshot and burning red. He coughed an awful lot and tried catching his breath. My mother said his health had been deteriorating although he tried making it out to be a cold. The atmosphere was ushered in complete silence by my mother's sudden appearance.

"Shouldn't you be off to school?"

I watered down a piece of pancake that had been in my mouth. "Yes ma'am." I could still feel a little food trapped in my throat, maybe because I didn't take the time to chew it.

"Then be gone, you shouldn't be sitting at this table still eating."

Victor turned to my mother and kissed her on the cheek, pulling her away from me at the same time. "Calm down, Evelyn, it's my fault. I made her a plate this morning. I forgot about the time."

She looked Victor seductively in his eyes and kissed him sweetly on his lips. "Don't let it happen again. I'm trying to teach her how to be punctual."

I shifted into maximum overdrive, grabbed the bulky textbooks on the table, and darted through the front door.

When I arrived at school, I entered the classroom and sat down at my desk, feeling dazed. Something warm and wet was underneath my bottom, covering me wholly, and when I raised myself a little, I could see it streaming down my leg. When I faced the ground, the bright fluorescent color put me in a state of shock. It became evident what I had done.

One of the classmates, Zora, whispered in her friend's ear, then shouted, "Ew, she's peeing on herself!"

Zora bullied me every day. Her shouts were loud enough for the whole class and the teacher to hear. In embarrassment, I grabbed my jacket, wrapped it around the back of my pants, trying to hide the big wet stain on the back and held up my index finger.

"Excuse me!"

Before I could run out, I had been caught by my teacher. This teacher hadn't been anything like my old one, Mrs. Bradley. The laughter made me feel like I was slowly dying inside.

"What's that on your leg?" Mr. Toner asked. He kneeled and pointed in the direction of my right leg with a ball point pen he'd removed from the pocket of his shirt.

I peeped an injured leg to see it bleeding. My skin was no longer there. I couldn't believe what

I was seeing and wanted to reach down and feel the area, but I'd heard about open wounds getting an infection if you touched it without washing your hands. It wasn't good either way, and the thought of it weakened my stomach. Only a chunk of meat was visible. It scared me so bad that I could feel myself becoming dizzy just from staring at the awful sight of it. It was pink and white in color.

Mr. Toner became quite concerned right away and pulled me outside the classroom into the hallway against the cream brick walls. I could still hear my classmates chattering with one another about me. It was an embarrassing moment, and one I wouldn't ever forget. The hardest question of my life was then asked.

"Is there anything going on at home? Has anyone been touching you?"

"What? No, everything is fine."

"Are you sure?"

I nodded, yes. With my back against the wall at that moment, I realized that it was the same position my mother always put me in at home. Mr. Toner waved principal Henton over, who then contacted the authorities.

Mr. Toner tried to give me some comfort, but I could feel none.

"I'm going to have to get in touch with your mother, okay?"

I begged him. "No, please don't do that."

He only looked at me, confused. "And why not? Are you afraid of your parents? I am your teacher, so you can talk to me, okay? You're bleeding, and we need to get you some help. Can you tell me who did that to you?"

So many questions flooded my brain all at once. I began to have flashbacks of my mother's beatings, her unfair and cruel punishments, and what transpired daily. I knew it would make things worse for me.

"Please, I beg of you, she mustn't find out."

"Who are you talking about dear, your mother?"

I told him that she'd been exactly who I was talking about. I was always told to go to school, do my work, and keep my mouth shut in public, as well. Mr. Toner walked back in class to gather something from his desk to take to nurse Randis' office. I peeked into the classroom and glanced over at Candice, who waved me goodbye with big bulging eyes.

When I got to the nurse's station, I drifted into a deep sound sleep topped with a major headache. I awakened, scared stiff by the uproarious tone of a masculine voice. The man was asking me a lot of personal questions. Most of all, this man, who wore a police uniform, told me that I was in safe hands. I could see my mother through the glass door, furious. "I demand to see my daughter!"

It didn't look good from her side. The officer let my mother speak to me for a small moment after she tried convincing them that I'd burned myself. The paramedics said it appeared to be a third-degree burn, that I couldn't have possibly suffered such a burn long enough to withstand it and not feel anything.

She slowly walked up to me. "I'm so tired of coming back and forth to this school having to get you for all these accidents. Now you have this unexplained burn mark on your arm! What happened?"

"Mama, I swear I don't know how it got there."

"Well, you'd better start thinking."

A paramedic walked in and stopped our conversation. "Ma'am, we've got to take her on to the hospital now."

The short plumpish-like paramedic commanded her away from me, and nurse Randis looked at my mother as if she were a suspect. She rubbed my forehead with watery eyes. I didn't know why she'd been crying for me. For a second, though, I felt like one of her own. She was confident that I'd be okay. Though I felt weak and lacked energy, I could still get around. Other parts of my body were going numb, and I fell asleep.

CHAPTER TEN

ST. FRANCIS BLUES

"I see you're awake. I'm Doctor Vontorrou. Do you remember the last thing that happened to you or anything at all?"

I looked to my right and noticed my father standing by me. I was in a hospital bed, and I didn't have a clue how I'd gotten there. The last thing I remembered was an officer and being hauled off by the paramedics.

"Not really," I said, tucking myself under the sheets. "I felt a little groggy this morning and then I ate breakfast."

He smiled and rested his hand on top of mine. "That's a good start for us. You have been showing signs of lethargy, and I had you hooked up for intravenous rehydration to make up for the fluids you've lost."

In my arm, there was an IV that gave off a stinging sensation whenever I moved it. "Ow!"

"Oh, careful there! You must keep your arm still. You have what we would call a seizure or an epileptic disorder. This is normally caused by abnormal electrical activities in the brain, so you will have to start seeing a neurologist very soon, okay?"

What was a neurologist? And where did this epileptic disorder come from? I wondered. Dr. Vontorrou explained to me that it could be hereditary after my mother told him we'd lost a few family members to it.

"I would also like to tell you, dear, that it's been the reason for the incontinence you've been having. It's usually one of the first signs."

My worries grew even stronger. "Will I be stuck this way?"

"I can't say. Studies have shown that some people outgrow their seizures, and with the right health care, anything is possible. So, always have faith, no matter the circumstances."

I caught a glimpse of my mother to my left bedside. I wasn't happy about seeing her. She looked dubious, standing there as if she were in a debate or trying to negotiate something with my father. I couldn't make out what or who it was they were carrying on about. It had to be me. I didn't know what she was doing here after tossing me out like I was garbage.

My parents tried to convince the doctor that I intentionally put the burn on my leg and that I might have developed a bipolar disorder. "Most times, when a person has a seizure, they'll lose consciousness," he replied. "They'll be unaware of what's happening around them. The burn is quite suspicious, yes, but it doesn't seem intentional."

Anyone would have screamed after putting heat to their skin, and if what my parents tried to get the doctor to believe were true, why hadn't they heard anything? Why hadn't they come running? How could someone my age withstand such pain? They had been displeased with me from the beginning. What parent would stoop so low as to degrade and make their child feel less in the eyes of others?

"May I ask who the child was with today?"

"She was with me and my husband all morning."

"Alright, I asked because there's going to be some investigation into this matter."

My mother's grip tightened at the shoulder strap of her handbag. "Fine."

I looked at her suspiciously, as she crouched down and wrapped her arms around my weak body, murmuring an excuse in my ear.

"I didn't know you had seizures, sweetie, and if I did, I wouldn't have whipped you so much." I broke down in a crying fit. I refused to believe any word she had to say. She'd never listened to me and never tried to figure out what was wrong for years until now. I was either too dramatic for her or overexaggerating things.

"Father, please don't send me back to live with her. I don't want to go back!"

"It's for the best. You and your mother need to work some things out."

How could I work something out with a mother who refused to meet me halfway? I tried to do nice things for her even when the holidays came around; I did what I could to make her happy. It never worked. She always made everything my fault.

"How do you know what's for the best?

No matter how much I begged, it was a done deal.

After being sent home from the hospital with the mysterious burn on my leg, my mother cared for it over the course of the months until surgery day approached. Doctor Vontorrou had ordered me to be sent for a skin graft procedure. After the surgical procedure, I was very weak and could hardly do anything for myself. The only reason my mother was being nice is that she'd been under investigation, but when that ended, things returned to how they were. The healing process took months on end, and I was still terribly saddened that my father sent me right back to live with my mother to endure more pain. He broke my heart before any other man could. My crown was leaning, with no one to straighten it. Only my pillow knows how many secrets I've hidden from the world to protect my parents.

CHAPTER ELEVEN

A PRISONER IN MY FATHER'S HOME

Things seemed to have died down for a while until I asked my mother if she could drop me off at the Cinemark Cinema 10 for my seventeenth birthday, and then that's when things went south. My epileptic disorder was brought up and that I couldn't be trusted to do things alone at the age of seventeen. I was still having a few seizures, which was becoming too much to bear for her. Every time she became enraged at me, she'd pick up the phone afterward, and that's when I knew I'd be getting sent away.

He pulled into the driveway, and it was just as I'd thought, a constant game of who-wants-the child that I'd become all too familiar with.

"Well, I knew it wouldn't be long before your mother came calling." My father gazed into the rearview mirror and slicked back his tide curls into a ponytail. "Ol' Evelyn just can't get enough of me coming around. I know she still misses me."

"She misses you. How?"

"You wouldn't understand. I think this time, you really got on her bad side. Your mom's a little crazy, something you'll see over time. So, you have to watch what you do around her."

He didn't have to tell me how she was. I already knew my mother had her issues like anyone else. He quickly changed from talking about my mother to having a conversation about how I would never be able to normally attend college like other students because of my seizures. He didn't bother talking to me about what career path I wanted to take because of it. I hated it when they talked about my illness as though I were some type of contagious lab rat that needed to be quarantined for the rest of her entire life.

"Why do you and Claire talk about me so bad?" I proudly questioned.

I wasn't afraid to ask, but tired of holding in what I'd been really wanting to let out since day one. My father kept driving without answering, and Claire unbuckled her seatbelt and turned around to face me, looking me dead in my eyes. "Don't you know that sometimes, it's better not to ask questions at all?"

She was just like my father, erupting with rage, but it didn't scare me.

"Well, I'm asking today because I need answers."

"Don't talk back, Miss Sassy!"

"I wasn't talking back."

Every time I tried to voice my feelings, I was always, if not later, shut down right away.

"You'd better get her Lawrence before I do because I'm going to pop her in the mouth."

My father placed his hand into hers and squeezed it tightly. "I'll handle her when we get home."

Claire always thought she was better than everybody because she was the daughter-in-law Grandmother Cara always liked and desired, and she had to be the center of attention. My father finally had someone that his mother truly accepted.

"Just look at you, your mama doesn't want you. That always leaves us to come get you every time. You're so unappreciative."

"What are you talking about? What have you really done for me that should warrant appreciation?"

I was hoping he'd jump in any second to protect me from Claire's crushing words. To cause injury to insult, he only joined in with her.

"You always have to get your point across, Tamara. Why can't you just learn to shut the hell up?" he asked.

"I...I.. was only speaking on how I felt."

I never felt loved or wanted, no matter where I went. My father went on to say how I would never have children, that they would be retarded or disabled. He said if I were somehow able to reproduce, it would be a miracle, and my children would make grunting noises all their lives. It was the most terrible thing to hear coming from my father, a parent's mouth in general. Instead of words of encouragement, he had shot me down. Claire was too tickled by his assertion. We came to a stop at a red light.

"You're lucky we don't just turn around and leave you with your mother," said Claire. Her smile was replaced with a scowl, and her cheeks aglow.

"Better there than being tormented like this," I responded.

"I'm just trying to teach you some things and prepare you for the future."

I hadn't been taught the right things that I should've known at my age. It was depressing enough not to be able to do what a lot of other young girls did at my age. My father wouldn't let me go anywhere near the kitchen, and he refused to teach me how to cook. They say it's a woman's job to teach a young girl her duties, and Claire hadn't put time into that department with me since I lived with them. They had even installed cameras inside the home to watch my every movement, which had been unexpected. I wasn't allowed outside and stayed trapped in a room with nothing but a bed and a television, and dinner was brought to me. When I asked why, he blamed it on my health. My meals were different than the twin boys; lunch mostly consisted of small melted ham and cheese sandwiches that became very tiresome.

When we got home, I walked straight inside to the house phone that was lying on the sofa and asked if I could call my mother. Of course, I found myself complaining about how he did things to her and Victor, who, on the other hand, never believed in anything my father did or said.

Once I'd finished talking with them and hung up the phone, I turned around to see my father standing there.

"Jeez, you almost scared me half to death. I didn't see you standing behind me."

He unplugged the cord from the phone jack and wrapped the cord around the phone. "I know you didn't. I have been listening to everything you've said. I don't approve of you telling what goes on in my house, and I would like you to go to your room and stay there until I let you out."

* * *

I was only telling them the truth, nothing more. After thinking about everything I'd been through living with my father, I waited until he wasn't around to creep out of my bedroom to the next room where the landline phone had been on a desk, still wrapped up perfectly. It would be noticeable if I plugged it back, so I didn't take the chance.

"You're going to get in trouble if you don't get out of here."

That voice! It was Jeremiah, and I turned around and ran to him, pleading with him not to tell Claire or my father.

"I just wanted to call my mother, that's it."

"I ain't gonna tell. Here's my cell; make it snappy."

"Thank you, little bro."

I took his phone into my hand and began secretly dialing shelters nearby to escape my father's wrath. The representative on the phone could tell I knew nothing about life behind the doors of a shelter, and she thought I was just one of those typical teenage runaways.

"Sweetheart, this isn't what you want to do."

"How can you tell someone what they don't want to do if you have never walked in that person's shoes and lived their journey?"

"Because sweetheart, there are people out there who really don't have homes and wish they did. If you leave home, you may regret it when you have to learn to survive in a world you're not prepared for."

She had no idea how badly I wanted to get away and the reasons that came with it. I was prepared to leave.

"Who are you on the phone with?"

My father's voice belted loudly throughout the room. Shocked, the phone dropped from my hand after finding he'd been listening in on me the entire time. My father shook me by the collar of my robe and dragged me to the living room, where Claire assisted him in tackling me to the floor.

He put both my arms and legs in some sort of wrestling hold that I couldn't free myself from.

Claire ran in, shouting, "What are you doing?"

"Stay the hell out of this and go back to your room!"

She jumped at his demands, and the twins came running out of their bedrooms. He kept me in a hold that had my body paining terribly. It would be a lesson that he was the only one that held the throne in his home and that nobody leaves him unless he gives permission. I was panting frantically, struggling to wriggle my body free. I couldn't seem to free myself, and I stared at the twins who looked onward in fear. I watched my father as he tied the belt from my robe around my arms and tightened it to keep me bound. They chose to keep out of it and ran back to their rooms. I laid there on the floor, demoralized. I wasn't allowed to leave his house unless I signed a power of attorney he placed right in front of my face, giving him full rights if something happened to me. I didn't think that the signature I'd place on that piece of paper would be another mistake I'd make just to set myself free. I finally broke free, flipping him on his back, and ran to my bedroom faster than a horse to a chariot that was set afire.

"Come back here, you little bitch!"

I hadn't realized my strength over a two hundred-eighty some pound man. I made my father very upset and as he tried forcing his way into the bedroom door I'd locked behind me, I looked for some place to get away. The security system he'd attached to my window after I tried running away before, sat waiting solid red and ready to alert if I ever tried to open it and escape again. That was the least of my worries because this time, I was going to make sure I left for good. I twisted both latches to my left and lifted the window. One could say I was more than bone tired, not being able to date, or even walk away from the yard to take a stroll without every move being watched. I could see that he was removing the doorknob from its hinges. I needed to move fast.

I was just one of those invisible girls, waiting for someone to pull me out of the darkness. Someone whose mother hadn't even had a talk with her about Aunt Flo until that day came, trapped in a box with no way out, no holes to breathe. I eased myself through the window, and the moment my feet touched the ground, I thought about what the representative on the phone said to me earlier. I would have to adapt and survive the streets if I chose to run away from both my parents forever. I ran until I reached a convenience store, and the clerk kindly let me use the phone to call who I needed. Somehow, I felt like I was backtracking into a nightmare that I intended to leave when I began dialing the numbers I hated the most, but what choice did I have?" I wasn't ready for what was out there.

"Hello?"

"Mom?" I began to muster up a whimper, and the phone trembled slightly against my ear. "Can you please come get me?"

I didn't know what else to do or who else to turn to. Most of all, I worried if my mother would hand me back over to my father. I had to wait until she arrived to see or if she would even come for me or leave me homeless.

CHAPTER TWELVE

2010

Time was passing us all by. I had obtained a decent paying job as an Administrative Assistant at Federal Express a year after I left my father's and maintained employment there for years. I met an attractive knockout on the job as well, whose name was Idris Se'Atkins, ruggedly handsome, muscular build and twenty-eight years old. I hadn't heard from my father since the day I ran away from him, and my mother took me back in after she and Victor had constantly been fighting with him. He changed his number and even stopped coming around the family. He wanted nothing more to do with Lawrence and me, and as far as Grandmother Cara knew, he moved away someplace with Claire and the twins and obtained a new identity. I was curious to know why he'd change his name and why he was so secretive about his whereabouts. Grandmother Cara would only say that some people just need that clean slate from the past, even though sometimes, the past tends to haunt you when you think you've got a fresh start.

"Happy born day! You're twenty-eight, and you look great! So, here you go." Victor smiled and handed me a black and gold gift bag. "How's my granddaughter?"

"Thank you. She's awesome and the best thing that ever happened to me."

"Glad to hear; I'd like to see my grandchild sometime," he simpered, "you should stop by the house on the weekends. Were always home unless we're going out on the town. You can bring her by then."

"I'll try."

I hadn't seen Victor or my mother since I'd given birth to my daughter and moved into my own apartment. Idris and I welcomed Liza together, who was now five years old. Over the years, I grew to like Victor, and so did Lawrence.

I didn't think I'd ever find it in me to like him. It took Lawrence a little more time. After a while, Victor began to show and teach us things that our father didn't bother doing. When my mother refused to teach me how to drive, Victor would take me to a church parking lot for a couple of practice rounds before he went off to work as long as I promised not to tell my mother. When my father or mother didn't bother teaching me how to cook, he also stepped in.

You know a wife isn't right if she doesn't know how to cook, and she's just as useless as a man who can't fix things, he would say. After that statement, I wanted to ask how he'd still been married to my mother. She didn't know how to cook. Apparently, it was in his facial expressions how much he'd grown apart from her.

"So, what's in the bag?" I asked.

Victor grinned and shook his head. "It wouldn't be a surprise if I told you now, would it?"

I chortled slightly and slowly removed some of the tissue paper wrapping from the bag.

"You're right."

Victor encouraged me with bloodshot eyes to open the gift that he'd gotten for me. I didn't think much of it, but that could've been the high blood pressure taking a toll on him again or the long work hours. I removed a Bible and a birthday card with a hundred dollar bill in it.

"Are you okay? Did you get enough sleep last night?"

"I'm alright, just a slight cold."

I tried focusing my attention on the gift but couldn't help noticing my mother sitting next to him, stuffing her mouth from a plate of delicious bar-b-que ribs. She hadn't spoken the entire time.

"I don't like to put anyone down by how they look, but from over here, you aren't looking very hot."

"I accept that." He took a sip of his sweet tea, then placed it back down. "We all grow old. Don't worry about me, Tamara; I'll be fine. Promise me one thing, though, that you won't make the same mistakes I did with your children and read your Bible."

I never saw his last response coming. Something was wrong, and I could feel it. My mother turned up her nose at me and looked away the more I questioned him.

That would be the last day I had a conversation with him, and my mother wouldn't have to worry about Victor anymore. He passed away a week later after my birthday due to natural causes of old age, so the doctor says. Some family members believed that he knew his time was coming. No one truly knows what happened the day he died because my mother refused an autopsy. She couldn't stand to be alone, so, six months after his death, she married for the third time.

SHAD'E ZUIWETA

CHAPTER THIRTEEN
THE CHURCH MEETING: PRESENT SITUATION

It was a late Friday evening, and I was attending a *married couples only* group session at New Rizer Fellowship with Idris on the West side of Monroe. I couldn't believe that as employees of the same company, we ended up marrying. I was told relationships on the job were bad luck. I believed in that, as one of my friends had a failed and dramatic work dilemma. We felt marriage was only right after we had Riza together and especially because of the love we had for one another.

"Hey, wait up a minute!" I searched my khaki pockets and pulled out my car keys. "I have to go back to the car to get our lesson books for tonight."

Idris stopped and waited for me as I returned to the car and spotted a rose gold decorated marriage ministry book labeled *couples living for and by God*, lying on the dashboard.

He never liked being surrounded by a huge crowd of people. After attending the group meeting a couple of times at the church, he was elated to go back a third. The church became a second home to us. The church's group leader, Rosser, always gave great compelling points in the meeting. Idris said it was quite a pleasant, if not an enjoyable experience, every time we went. I was hesitant myself in the beginning, as we were the only interracial couple and had been new to the group. I had just gotten off work with only a small window to make it inside and on time for the meeting. I did my best to hurry into the building, interrupted by my phone's ringer.

"Dammit, why is she calling so much?" I said, not realizing I'd shouted it out loud.

Idris walked up, concerned, and asked, "Who's that calling?"

"No one, just my mother."

She had called numerous times for Liza. I had no time to speak. It was more so that I didn't want to speak with her at all, so I tapped the decline button and headed into the building.

"Let's go before they lock the doors."

My phone buzzed again. It had been her calling right back. This time, she left an unpleasant voicemail, demanding to speak with Liza. I powered off my phone, and we settled into a small room of twelve, listening to all the wonderful testimonies in the room like soldiers wounded, but were survivors by the grace of God.

Everyone soon gathered around the associate pastor in hard black plastic chairs, ate fruit, and laughed hysterically at the jokes he made, as he spoke on the five love languages. The members of the group gave him their undivided attention. He tried his best to comfort those who were scarred; still, he could tell it was hard for some to keep the pain at bay. I knew because I was one of them.

After the meeting ended, I went to the associate pastor and asked, "Why me? How do you walk up to someone you've cared about and known for so long to tell them that they have left a certain mark on your heart when they refuse to listen?"

The pastor, with tight eyes but a solemn expression, responded, "I'm sorry for what you've encountered and for the things that you've had to go through. Sometimes, when we care too much for someone more than they deserve, we tend to get less than what we deserve in return." Though I was put on edge by what he said, I took it as a lesson learned. I was always that loving person who put in way too much, too fast, to please those who cared nothing about my needs, leaving me abandoned in the end. I wondered where God was through the pain and suffering. It felt like sharp needles poking at my skin every time I tried to get away for healing. Like others I'd told, he reassured me that everything would be alright.

"Babe, could you please pass me that pen next to you?"

Idris handed me the pen, and I took out a small notepad from my purse. I loved taking notes during the meeting. Afterward, I'd go straight to my notepad when we got home and read over the important things I'd jotted down. I picked up my Bible and read Psalm 31:13-15. It touched my heart in so many ways and gave me much encouragement as I read it. With the Bible gripped tightly in the palm of my hands as though it were about to slip, I read the heartfelt words aloud.

For I hear many whispering, terror on every side! They conspire against me and plot to take my life, but I trust in you Lord; I say, "you are my God.

How could I not want to carry these words with me? I was a woman who suffered an unimaginable pain throughout the years at the hands of her parents.

Every time I tried my hardest to move on with my life, there was something with the past and the present that intertwined. Once the meeting was over, I turned my phone back on, and immediately, the ringer, which sounded like chiming bells, went off in the room. I was so irritated by her constant calling that I answered.

"Yes, mother?"

"Where's my baby? Is she well?"

"You mean my daughter? And why do you keep asking all these crazy questions every time you call, like she isn't in good health?"

"Because she's my granddaughter. I have a right to know! Why won't you let me talk to her? You know I'll make you regret every part of this. Watch me!"

The irate tone of my mother's voice brought me back to those childhood memories that I couldn't seem to escape, showing that she had always been on a short fuse and could barely contain herself. She hadn't changed. She had gotten on my nerves more and more over the years. I was due for baby number two, another daughter in a few months. She never bothered to congratulate or show any interest in being a part of Liza's life until I married Idris.

I was sick and tired of her always wanting to know my whereabouts, what I was doing in my household with my husband, and if my child was healthy every time she called like I was the neglectful mother she had been to me. Ever since I left her home at eighteen, she'd had it in her blood to tear me down. She never wanted to see me have children, and neither did my father, as they both told me I wouldn't. She hadn't even given me a wedding gift- a wedding she never wanted to come to in the first place, that I begged her to attend.

"Look, Liza is my child! And I know you aren't really concerned about my child or the one that's coming. Goodbye!"

In a fraction of a minute, the call disconnected. This was nothing new with her when it came to the heated arguments between us. I looked over my shoulders every time I went around her, believing that if I didn't keep my eyes open, my mother would intentionally hurt or poison me someday when I least expected it. I hated how my heart felt about her. I needed to talk to someone about those feelings besides Idris, so I talked to my Grandmother Cara about everything. My mother was set in her own ways and hated me for marrying Idris because of his race and political beliefs that were far different than hers. I wish we didn't live in a world where everything was based on that. Unfortunately, we do. I didn't care how my mother or my family felt about him. I was deeply in love with Idris, and he was with me. Race was never an issue, like it is for some.

CHAPTER FOURTEEN
GRANDMOTHER CARA

I drove around and looked at my old apartment, unit 207 at the Camden one last time. It had been my very first apartment and the place I'd been living before Idris and I married. I took a moment of silence to take in how far I'd come and how hard I'd worked, especially as my parents had told me I'd never be able to do anything. I was now living in an upscale and beautiful home in a nice quiet neighborhood with my husband and children. I was happy to have my own little family. Things were peaceful now that I was finally shown love and protection from someone who truly cared.

* * *

I hadn't spoken to my Grandmother Cara in a long time. She had just come back from vacationing and celebrating her eighty-ninth birthday in Honolulu. Since falling out with my father, I decided to reach out to her a few weeks after she came back to town. Liza would finally be able to spend some time with her, and my Grandmother Cara could soon meet our youngest daughter, Mariyah, for the first time. She would be arriving in a few months. Grandmother Cara had always been a well-respected woman, and many knew her to be sociable with almost anyone, who would give you the best advice if you seriously needed it. I could count on her for almost anything, and if I needed a favor, more than likely, she would get right on it if she weren't busy in the streets with her friends. She took a lot of luxury vacations that left a strain on Uncle Levy's pockets at times. He did anything he could to make his mother happy because my father wasn't going to do it. She always said you only get one life, so you might as well live it to the fullest and party like it's your last. Even though I looked up to her, she could never compare to my sweet grandmother Helen. She was now battling Alzheimer's and barely remembered who I was or any of the family members when we came to visit her.

"Hey baby, it's so nice to hear from you."

She was astounded to hear my voice after so long, and knew I was always the type that liked to stay to myself. I was working and in college, studying Healthcare Administration for the most part. She always rambled on that everyone forgot about her and that she hadn't heard from my brother or my father in years.

"I can't ever get your brother to call me, and here you are." She spread her arms out. "Come, give your grandma a hug."

I put my arms around her, and she pulled me closer in a tight bear hug. I could feel the excitement, and when she mentioned she couldn't get in touch with Lawrence, I knew that he was just taking some time to deal with the letdown that our father had gone again. He preferred not to talk to anyone. The hate he once had for Victor, he'd lashed out in the hatred for our father, but not for the faults of our mother as well.

"It's so wonderful to see that you've settled down and gotten married, and your family, oh, you guys are so beautiful together."

"Yes, I did, and he's the best man a woman could hope for."

"That's really good. I wish your cousin Mona could've been more like you; she's always running around here with these thuggish little boys getting drunk and staying in trouble all the time."

I listened to her talk about Mona, who was her favorite granddaughter, for twenty minutes. Next, she moved on to my father until I stopped her and asked if Liza could stay and spend time with her for the week.

"It's our anniversary, and I'm not on good terms with my mother right now."

"Oh, baby, I hate you two are still going through the same thing. I thought by now, your mama would have stopped that nonsense. No worries, I'll keep Liza for you. She needs to spend time with me anyway."

I rose from the sofa and hugged her again. "Thanks a lot! If you need anything, just let me know."

"Alright, I wish that everyone would just get along."

I felt this would be a good opportunity for my daughter to bond with the woman I grew up around. I could hear my cell phone vibrating, but I didn't bother answering it. It was probably only my mother.

"Sweetheart, this is your great grandmother, Cara. You may not remember her because you were just a small baby at the time. You're going to be staying with her for the week until your father and I get back from our vacation, okay?"

"Okay. Love you, Mommy."

"I love you more. Behave, and do what she tells you to do."

"Don't worry your paws about anything. Go on and have yourself some fun," Grandmother Cara said.

"You know, I will. Please, if for any reason my mother calls, trying to talk with Liza, don't let her."

"You don't have to worry about anything. I know how your mother is and how she was with you guys when you were younger. Go on and enjoy yourself."

She opened the front door, and I waved Liza goodbye. When I got back home, Idris and I packed our luggage, loaded up and rushed to the airport for our flight to Miami, Florida. Little did we know that leaving my daughter with my father's mother, who I thought I could trust, would be the greatest mistake I'd ever made in my life.

CHAPTER FIFTEEN

ALL IN THE FAMILY

When Idris and I finally returned from our anniversary trip, Liza rushed into my arms and hugged me as if she hadn't seen me in years.

"Mommy! I had so much fun with Nana Cara."

I took her into my arms and squeezed her tightly. "You did? That's awesome!"

"Here is Liza's belongings. How was the trip?"

"It was lovely," I replied. "I'm sure I don't even have to explain. You've been to Miami more than I have. Thank you so much for watching her, and if you need anything or any more food, then let Idris or I know. We'll get it for you."

We always brought my grandmother Cara food anytime she needed it when no one else in the family would bother stopping by, besides Uncle Levy, to make sure she was good on essentials.

"Speaking of food, I'm going to need some coleslaw, sweet potato salad, yogurt parfait, and a few other things. I'm low on those," she replied, "but I will let you know for sure this weekend once I have the full list."

It had only been a few short hours since I'd left her house, and my phone rang. "Yes, hello?"

"Am I speaking with Mrs. Se'Atkins?"

"Speaking, who is this?"

"My name is Ms. Bowers, and I'm a social worker from the Child Protection Services Agency. I suggest you meet with me at once, or I'll have the authorities at your house!"

I was shocked to find out that I'd been contacted by a very rude and anxious social worker. She hadn't even given me a chance to speak. One demand came after another, and she accused me of abuse and neglect to Liza. My right hand clung to my belly as the other kept steady on the wheel. I began to move my hand in a circular motion to keep myself from panicking, trying to figure out who could've made a false report on me against my own child. I had been abused, and there was no way I wanted my children to suffer that same pain.

"Please, do not call my phone being disrespectful. There's a right way to do things, and then there's a wrong way."

The social worker was already pointing fingers and had not even met me yet or investigated the false rumors. To my understanding, she'd already been to my daughter's school and interrogated her. I could feel my heart pounding, wondering if my daughter had been taken unlawfully by this woman.

"Well, regardless, we need to talk. I'm headed straight for your house, and if you don't meet me there, I will contact the authorities, and your child will be removed!"

"With your attitude, I don't think so."

I hung up and dialed Idris right away to meet me at Liza's school. I was surprised to see he'd beaten me there. I began to praise the man upstairs when I saw Liza at his side. She hadn't been taken, and her face was flushed with cherry dots.

"Goodness! What's wrong with her face? It looks like she has a rash, and where's her teacher?"

"She's fine. She was in recess outside when I checked her out. The teacher said her nose had been running an awful lot, and her eyes were watery as well while she was running around with the other students. It's just allergies."

"Alright."

"I hope you know this is your parents' doing. We need to meet this social worker and see what she has to say about Liza."

I called the social worker back and agreed to meet her. She came to my house and read off a long report that immediately brought my attention to my parents, then she questioned Liza alone about the false allegations and threatened to contact the authorities about a bruise that was visible on her right arm.

She stepped up to me, holding a folder to her chest compressed with multi-colored papers and snarled at me.

"If your daughter isn't being abused, then why does she have that bruise on her arm?"

"Ms. Bowers, is it? My daughter has a bruise on her arm, yes, but who's to say where that came from? You act as if children aren't active and don't get scars, scratches, and bruises throughout their lives. If you have children, you would know that."

I was agitated and worked up and requested that the social worker leave my residence. Instead of listening, she acted like my parents. I knew the allegations were my parents' doing. They were just alike, and I knew after so long, that my father had come back to ruin me, as he said he would do. He not only had it out for me but Idris this time, as well.

I demanded my father stay away from my family and me the day he'd contacted me after so many years, wanting to see my children. I had finally stood up and cut the lifeline between my mother and me as well. The disconnection angered them both. We were constantly dealing with the child protection service worker daily, and several other reports that followed. We knew it was always them every time, and so did my grandmother Cara when I discussed the matter with her over the phone.

"I'm sorry you're going through this with Evelyn and your father. I told your mother when she called over here for Liza not to call those people, but she did it anyway."

"What do you mean?" My back was hunched over, and the phone clenched tightly in my hand.

"You knew she planned to call the CPS, and you didn't tell me?"

"I'm sorry, baby. I pleaded with her not to call those people. She said Liza was being treated unfairly, that she was in danger, wearing dirty clothing, not eating. You get the picture?"

I rubbed my head. Somehow, I could feel a migraine creeping up on me. This information weighed down heavily on my soul, and my suspicions were confirmed. I couldn't bear to hear anymore. Neither could I stomach the pain of my own family doing this to me, knowing that my daughter was truly healthy.

"Grandma, you know how I treat my daughter. She's always dressed decently, and she had clean clothing when she spent time with you."

My parents wanted to make me look like a horrible parent, and they were doing a hell of a job at it. My daughter was a beautiful little girl with loving parents, and anyone who knew me could attest that Liza was in a nurturing environment. Grandmother Cara had shed more light on my mother than she did her own son. I felt awful that my husband had to be brought in the middle of such dramatic and dysfunctional family members. We don't get to pick and choose our family members. If it were possible, I'd be the first in line to put in a request for a different family. Nevertheless, Idris always lifted my head every time and reassured me that nobody's family was perfect and that his family had some flaws, although not as bad as mine. I had to laugh a little at that because it had been true. I loved this man for being there for me every day. My family was making things so bad for us that they were hoping we'd argue, fight, and then divorce. Though my grandmother Cara told me my mother had been behind the reports, there was an uncanny feeling that something else was amiss.

"Thank you for being such a listening ear, Grandma. I got the food you've been asking for, and if you would like to pick it up, it'll be sitting right here on the table."

"Awesome, I'll get by there this weekend to get it. I have to go now," she murmured.

Something about her had been odd. Every time we were on the phone, she'd hurry me off the phone, like she no longer liked talking to me anymore.

"Hey, by the way, I want to ask you a few questions."

"Yes, dear?"

"Did Liz ever talk to my mother during the duration of her stay with you?"

"No! Now you know I would never go against your word like that. She never talked to Evelyn at all. She stayed here, played video games and watched movies the whole time. Your mother only called once, but I was the only one that talked to her."

I had known my grandmother Cara basically all my life. I knew when she was lying to me, and this had been one of the moments she chose to. My husband and I had given her everything, and I'd felt comfortable enough to open a jar of feelings to her. Now she was lying straight to my face, with a gut feeling telling me she had done so. I told her I would call her right back and shouted for Liza to come downstairs, and she came running with a smile perked on her face.

"Yes, Mommy?"

"Do you remember Grandmother Cara?"

"I do."

"Well, could you tell me if you did anything exciting besides playing games with her. Go anywhere interesting or talk to certain people while you were there?"

"Yeah! I saw my Grandma Evelyn and Grandpa, and they were mad. Not with me, but you, and they said I wouldn't be living with you too much longer."

It seemed strange that she didn't mention this before when we were at my grandmother Cara's. I thought she'd told me all about her stay, but even children can be told to keep secrets. I knew the truth all along, and I had been right. I trusted Grandmother Cara with all my heart and had even invited her into our home multiple times. In her, I confided my troubles, and things that were currently going on with Ms. Bowers, the child protection service worker, and she turned right around and misused the information and placed it straight into the hands of my father, mostly, to twist around for his own personal gain.

"You knew of the abuse I sustained at my parent's hands and how I never wanted them around my children, but you let them around my daughter anyway. You knew they were plotting against me. You also asked Liza not to tell me she had been talking with my mother. What else are you not telling me? Did you take Liza to see those abusive tyrants?"

"Your daughter is lying. I never took her anywhere. How could you believe that child over me?"

"That child you're referring to is my daughter. I can sense when she is lying and telling the truth, and most of all, I know when you aren't."

"You're making me mad right now, and I don't like to be mad."

"Good! I love you, and I don't know the reasoning behind your lying, but this is where I draw the line!" I said, tapping the edge of the smooth, polished coffee table.

Nothing but total silence traveled through the phone, and then came hard breathing. I lowered my phone. There was nothing more to say to her; trust was out the door. It's true what they say. Sometimes, a listening ear is nothing more than a running mouth. I was worn out in my mind and in my soul. Saddened, I chose to distance myself from her as well, and, shortly after the call, kneeled in prayer. Though I had been depleted of so much energy, I was not going to give up so easily on this fight. My husband was devastated, not only by what my family had done to me but to him as well. He was even more upset that after all these years, and throughout the fight of our children with the agency, Lawrence had chosen to step back and stay out of it. He hadn't come forward and spoken on my behalf of how good of a mother he knew me to be.

My parents had taken us on an uphill battle of countless CPS reports. I never asked for any of this and wished many years ago that I had not let them have so much control over me. They were on a path of retaliation and destruction, and they weren't going to stop until both my children were taken from me.

I was always a hoe, dumb, or something beyond that in my father's eyes. My mother should've been his long-term sidekick instead of Claire. I didn't deserve the rude CPS worker knocking at my door or any of what they put me through when I always kept my head in my books and made men the last resort in my life. Why couldn't they be proud of me like other parents?

The more they called those social workers on me to say I abused Liza, the more injurious it was to her. They didn't care how she felt. With every visit, she was becoming emotionally damaged by the questions she was asked. *In her I saw me. She was that same little girl being questioned, but the only difference here was that my little girl wanted for nothing; her mother was innocent and tried to break a cycle her family created.*

I held my Bible close to my heart and sung that sweet melody my grandmother Helen used to sing while she rocked in her wooden porch swing to calm her nerves and worries.

I gave a piece of me just to be crushed repeatedly, but life is but a game we play to win, and though I feel weak, I know I'm strong, and it's gonna be, gonna be alright.

CHAPTER SIXTEEN
BLOOD ISN'T ALWAYS THICKER

The vexatious allegations were beginning to take a toll on my family one by one. The household duties, the demands of my employer, and taking care of the new baby, along with the stressful child protection service workers coming in and out of our home, were increasingly onerous. I took my beautiful bubbly daughter and cradled her in my arms. Her smile glowed beautifully when I looked into her chestnut eyes. I couldn't imagine harming her or Liza like my parents told everyone I had.

Idris sat down at the table and rolled back his sleeves. "Everything's going to be alright. Don't try to dwell on it too much."

"I hope so," I responded, caressing his hand that had been resting beside his plate.

This is just what they wanted, for me to give up on my family and run back to them.

Narcissists love to feel wanted and, most of all, needed. In everything my parents did, they couldn't see the wrong they'd done. I didn't need them; they needed me. I had done my research earlier, and learned narcissists target specific people, the strong-willed and talented. I was a survivor, and that's what made me surpass their level. Though I did have struggles here and there, I never really begged anyone for anything. They judged me for so much when I always did my job as a mother.

Idris and I finally rose from the table after we had eaten and emptied the scraps from our plate. We put our dishes in the sink when we suddenly heard a knock at the door. I opened it and was immediately questioned by a man in a black and white button-down, black pants suit.

"Is your name Tamara?"

I began scratching the back of my head. "Um, yes, and who are you?"

"Just here to do my job, ma'am. This belongs to you."

He handed me a stack of papers and walked away before I had a chance to ask him what it was I was holding. I wished I'd asked who wants to know instead of volunteering my name.

Glancing at the papers that were handed to me, I was dumbfounded to see it was an order of protection. It had been taken out on my husband and me by Claire and my own father out of spite. I'd already been through so much, now this? The horrible things that were stated in the order of protection were damaging and falsified. I don't know what parent in the world would ever do such a hateful thing in their life to take attention away from their own behavior to play the victim. In the report, it said we both physically attacked him. My father was clever and brilliant. He knew he wouldn't be able to obtain the order against us unless he lied to say we attacked him, and he did just that. He would stop at nothing until he hurt me and gained control again, something I refused to give him. They would never let me heal from the past that I'd tried to lay to rest. It kept finding its way back to me. I immediately picked up my phone and dialed my mother to tell her what had just happened.

"Did you know he was going to do this? And what about the CPS? Were you all with them on that? You can't deny it!" I asked.

"Do you know what time it is? You're disturbing my sleep," she moaned. "Your husband must've put you up to questioning me? I told you not to marry him. You seem to like those types, though. Yeah, I know who called, but I can't tell you who did it, and I didn't know he was going to take out a restraining order against you."

I banged my fist on the table and jumped to my feet from the chair I'd been sitting in. "Lies! What kind of mother has so much hate for her child that she plots or becomes an accomplice to destroy that child? Why would you even keep things like this from me? I know it was the both of you!"

Once law enforcement is involved, there is no letting you back into my life or around my children, no matter who you are. When I finally chose to speak my mind after all these years, family turned on me as well, and I got knocked right back down for it, physically attacked even as an adult. Since Victor's passing, they had become a team. Basically, helping one another along with Claire to do away with me for good so that I could no longer have access to my children if I violated the order of protection.

I admit that I had my share of being infuriated with my mother in the past, speaking out of anger and frustration because of the abuse I'd sustained in the past, but I would have never done to her what she did to me. What hurt most of all is that no one ever apologized to me, and I knew my parents were never going to do that. My mother told several people that I was a mistake, and she often reminded me of that whenever she grew angry with me. She wished she could undo it all, and so did my father, not caring what others would say about their poor choice of words and whether it would pang me. I could have never imagined saying that to any of my children, no matter how mad they made me.

"Of course, you'd say such nasty things. I'd fight for my children before I let you or anyone else put their hands on my children."

"I don't know why you can't let the past go!" She yelled.

"And I don't know why people like you constantly say that when you've never walked in or lived the pages of my story. You say nasty things and try to get my children taken away from me. I will fight for mine before I let you or anyone else lay a hand on them."

Not many will know how it feels to have two parents against you and not fully know the reasons behind their intentions. I could hear people in the background telling my mother what to say. I wondered if my brother had played a part in that.

"I wasn't able to conceive the child I always wanted with Victor. You have two children now just as I do, and you won't have any more than that. I can give them better."

My heart began to sink by those jarring words. "Goodbye, mother, the hell in which you live will be the hell that overwhelms you."

I hung up in her face, not giving her any more chances to spill another lie and say another negative word. I flung the door of my master bathroom open in a rage, stricken by what my own mother had just said to me. I turned the knobs of my tub and watched the water fill halfway to the top. I stepped in and began to soak in a bubble-filled pomegranate and berry-scented bath, accompanied by organic salts. It was a much-needed bath that felt relaxing to both my mind and body spiritually. Idris walked in and began massaging my back, working his way from the middle down to my bottom, hitting the spot right where it hurt. I asked him a question in hopes he could provide an answer. "Hon, when will it be my time to see justice? When will my mother be held accountable for her actions?"

He slumped down next to me, leaning against the tub and responded, "Sometimes, sweetheart, bad people tend to have better luck than those who are good. It takes time, but justice will prevail." He winked and placed a dry towel at my side.

CHAPTER SEVENTEEN
INJUSTICE

Idris and I prepared ourselves for court the following Tuesday morning. We entered the courtroom and sat down on hard wooden benches. The man that I used to call my father before I'd decided to disown him was walking in to testify against me. With him came Claire, my mother, and my Grandmother Cara, who I hadn't expected to be at his side. My mother's new husband, Augustus, was close behind as her supporter.

"Do you swear to tell the truth, the whole truth, and nothing but the truth, so help you, God?"

I inhaled slowly. "I do."

One of my hands fell softly on the Bible the Bailiff placed before me, the other raised solemnly in the air as we held genuine and sincere eye contact. I stood bold, prepared for the challenges that awaited me. I was not afraid. I'd done no wrong. However, I loved and let the wrong people stay in my life for too long. Everyone looked my way as I moved precipitously to tuck my silenced phone away. It was a betrayal, for sure that my mother knew, that kept her from meeting my eye.

"Sir, why is it that you and your wife seek a permanent order of protection against the defendants?"

"My daughter has attacked me in public, and because of that, I fear for my safety. We are also desperate to have some type of safety net put in place from the threats these two have instilled upon my wife's life. She is sickly and can do very little for herself."

My father had readily prepared the perfect speech beforehand. It was well thought out, and he could've gotten three Oscar nominations for it that day. It was jaw-dropping for Idris and I to hear how good of a liar he was. We knew from how well he played the victim role that he'd have Judge Whitman pitying him and falling for his story in no time. It wasn't until that moment that we agreed we should've hired an attorney. Before the court date, Idris was confident that we didn't need one. There was no way we were prepared for the fabricated documents he handed the judge.

"Is there anything else you'd like to say, sir?" said Judge Whitman, taking the gavel into his hand.

"What about what we have to say?"

I interrupted Judge Whitman and he stared with a pinched expression of annoyance, brows drawn inward, breathing noisily, as though he were about to snap.

"Do not interrupt me! You will have your turn in a moment!"

"Yes, I do have one more thing I'd like to say, actually." My father held Claire's hand and helped her join him at the podium where he was standing. "We ask that you hold them in contempt for violating the temporary order of protection. They were outside of our home, and I have the defendant's mother here as a witness to this."

"He's lying!" I shouted.

My parents had taken things to the extreme. Idris was as surprised as I was. I couldn't believe how crazy they were to escalate the situation in only the short period of time we'd been in court. Their motive was now clear. First, the child protection service (CPS) workers had been sent to our doorstep. They saw that that hadn't worked out in their favor, that the social worker saw nothing but kind and loving parents with vindictive family members. The worker even confessed to me that many calls to CPS were often made in spite. Why not improve your system to catch people like this then? When their attempts to criminalize us using calls to CPS, my father and Clair took a different route: they obtained a false order of protection to make both Idris and I look like criminals in the eyes of everyone.

"I will not grant you that, but what I can do is grant you the permanent order of protection that you seek. Mr. and Mrs. Se'Atkins, if you violate this order, you will go to jail. The two of you must stay away from each other."

Judge Whitman looked at us as though we had truly committed an act of violence against the plaintiffs. He immediately empathized with them and had the Bailiff assist Claire, who was rubbing her forehead and pretending she was about to faint.

"Are you okay, ma'am? Would you like a drink of water?" the Bailiff asked generously.

"Oh, I think I'll be alright, but I do feel a bit hot."

Hatred for my father ran so deep. He wasn't even man enough to attend my wedding—his only daughter's wedding. He fabricated excuses for everything, and Claire had always been in the middle of it. He never walked me down the aisle. I didn't expect him to, but I knew if Victor had been alive, he would've loved to. Even though my father had walked out on me, out of the goodness of my heart, I still invited him to my wedding and even my baby shower. Now this is what I got in return. My mother was hesitant to attend as well. I never even received a bridal gift from either them, which was sad. However, I never confronted them about it. My mother always thought I'd never settle down with a well-respected gentleman who made a decent living for himself. I proved her wrong. No one can determine your future.

The judge dismissed everything I said and never granted me my rightful turn to speak. When I questioned him on this, I was told there was no need for either Idris or myself to speak any further. Idris and I were allowed to speak only once in our defense, while my father slandered my name as he pleased, numerous times. It was an unfair ruling that left me devastated and screaming inside. In that moment, my life was replaying my childhood: no one could hear me shouting for help, and I was drowning. I watched as Judge Whitman ruled in favor of the true abuser and dismissed the court session. No matter what anyone thinks, the system did indeed fail me horribly. I tried to emphasize the evidence in our defense, arguing that things were not what he made them out to be; even with the recordings, I tried to tell him that I had to refute my father's claims. My father's testimony was his only proof, so the order said. Idris and I were both ordered to pay court costs for everyone who attended.

"Does anybody have any questions?"

I slammed my fist on the podium before me. "You've got to be kidding me; you bet I have a question!"

"And what is that?" the judge rudely replied.

"You let him speak multiple times and said we would have our chance to as well. We were not given that, only once. Where's the justice in that?"

"Because you don't deserve to speak."

I was dumbstruck. I'd been shot down and victimized all over again. Judge Whitman dismissed me without another thought, banging his gavel and calling in his next case. I respect authority, but what I can't respect is authority that refuses to see the truth. Respect is a two-way street. My father loved Claire. She was who he always wanted to be with and who he wanted children with, not my mother. He'd moved from a position of disinterest to one of malevolent vengeance and control.

My mother bolted for the courtroom door and tried not to look my way. She collapsed before getting her foot out, and the officers ran to her aid. I stood nearby, watching her convulse. I could feel my heart breaking, watching her, but a part of me held back from reaching out. Maybe now she could feel some of my pain and suffering, as she laid there helpless. This was a day where I was powerless to prevent injustice—an unjust day in court—but I promised myself I would stop at nothing until it was served. I would place it all in the hands of the Most High.

EPILOGUE

The year was now 2014, and that court battle
was now one year in the past. My mother had
fully recovered from her body excessively
overheating, and Claire had passed away from a
brain aneurism in bed on an early Saturday
morning. It seems she had been sick in court, and
he used that as an excuse. No one really knew
how sick she was until she passed away; it was
then that people realized my father had been too
ashamed to tell everyone he was losing the
person that meant the world to him to cancer.
Shortly after, he filed for bankruptcy and, from
what Lawrence told me, moved away again.

Idris smiled and swooped my hair behind my
ear. "You look absolutely beautiful. Are you
ready?"

Grinning from ear to ear, I sharped to his left
in a gorgeous satin gown. "I've been ready."

His arms wrapped tightly around my hips, and
it was there he told me that he'd never stopped

loving me or believing in me throughout all the struggles, that I'd do great on stage, and after it was all over, he'd be waiting for me just as he had at the altar.

He was always such a sweet and uplifting man, and I appreciated him greatly. As we held each other close, Idris explained that he never had the best of parents either. The pain that I endured was similar to the pain he encountered because of his father.

Our home had endured the fiercest battles. We knew that a family that prayed together would stay together, and we were determined to with everlasting love. It took losing a lot of people I once trusted to show me they weren't meant to be kept in the first place.

I walked on stage courageously, equanimous in posture, as the crowd raised their hands and cheered. The way my jaw hurt when I smiled showed me that I hadn't smiled that big in a long time. I had finally moved on to become prosperous, and I was proud of myself. They had not been successful in tearing down my home, though they still try to this day. I tapped the microphone to test it, as my speech weighed heavy in my heart.

Good evening everyone, my name is Tamara Se'Atkins. I am one of many people who have been physically and verbally abused throughout my childhood and adult life. I was manipulated and taken advantage of by the very same people I first laid eyes on when I came into this world: my parents. Though I was told I'd never become anything, that I'd be different from others, I was determined to become someone. I finally told myself that different is better. You stand out! I have now been seizure-free for years, and I stand before you today a survivor of this all, and you can be that too.

I could see Idris front row and center, clapping a very happy well done. He waited for me at the bottom of the staircase, his hand held out and a bouquet of beautiful mixed red and white roses in the other; their gratifying scent sweetly filled the air around us. He gingerly escorted me toward the auditorium, where it was just the two of us, and I thanked him with a kiss. I felt a safe harbor away from all other things as he congratulated me further.

"There is one last thing that I ask of you despite the storm: forgive your mother, not for her benefit, but for your heart and sanity, so that we can walk through those golden gates of heaven hand in hand when the time comes."

He waited for a response that would probably never come. I was so angry inside for being repeatedly looked at as the criminal when I was really the victim. The system was designed to protect innocent people. It hadn't done that for me.

I replied, "I can forgive, but I cannot forget. There's no way I'd be stupid enough to trust them with my heart anymore."

I wanted revenge. However, they were already suffering. From a distance, God let me watch what he had in store, on full screen and in high definition. I was satisfied with that. I felt it in my soul that he was working through his own justice system. *Wounds heal, but scars remain. And as far as Karma, well, it never loses an address!*

ABOUT THE AUTHOR

Shad'e Zuiweta is a wife and mother of two and her curious canine. Zuiweta has always had a passion for writing and singing since the age of seven. She is affiliated, and a proud member of the Author's Guild and currently at work on a romantic suspense novel. Want more from this author?

Facebook.com/Shad'e Zuiweta

Instagram.com/Shad'e Zuiweta